Adele PARKS

LOVE IS A JOURNEY

headline
review

A selection of these stories were published in the digital collections *Finding The One*, *Love Is Complicated*, *New Beginnings* and *Happy Endings*

An extended credits page can be found on page 260 and 261

The right of Adele Parks to be identified as the Author of the Work has been asserted by her in accordance with the Copyright, Designs and Patents Act 1988.

First published in this collected edition in Great Britain in 2016 by
HEADLINE REVIEW
An imprint of HEADLINE PUBLISHING GROUP

5

Cataloguing in Publication Data is available from the British Library

ISBN 978 1 4722 4051 4 (paperback)

Typeset in Monotype Dante by Palimpsest Book Production Limited, Falkirk, Stirlingshire

Printed and bound in Great Britain by
Clays Ltd, St Ives plc

Headline's policy is to use papers that are natural, renewable and recyclable products and made from wood grown in sustainable forests. The logging and manufacturing processes are expected to conform to the environmental regulations of the country of origin.

HEADLINE PUBLISHING GROUP
An Hachette UK Company
Carmelite House
50 Victoria Embankment
London, EC4Y 0DZ

www.headline.co.uk
www.hachette.co.uk

This book is dedicated to Catherine Divers, Katie King, Michelle Ratcliffe, Vicky-Leigh Sayer, Rachel Simm and Stephanie Talmage.

Contents

'Love is too magnificent to be controlled by a rationale or even a rule, however well-intentioned that rule is. Maybe love is about the messy bits too. Jealousy might be part of love. It might be an essential part.'

Rich, *Still Thinking of You*

'Love is a good thing.'

Laura, *Husbands*

'Love is such a responsibility.'

Lucy, *Young Wives' Tales*

'Love is a really hard habit to kick. So before you ask, I'm not going to leave him.'

George, *Larger Than Life*

'Your love is my life.'

Luke, *Playing Away*

'I don't think unconditional love is a possibility never mind a probability.'

Cas, *Game Over*

'Love isn't something to be afraid of.'

Tash, *Still Thinking of You*

'Love is the only thing that counts.'

Philip, *Husbands*

'Love is quite extraordinary in its capacity to forgive.'

Rose, *Young Wives' Tales*

'True love is all absorbing. It's possible to be curious, infatuated, wistful, maybe.'

Amelie, *Husbands*

'Love is accepting the person, faults and mistakes and all.'

Fern, *Love Lies*

'You were wrong, Karl, sex isn't everything. Love is everything. I want her back'.

Neil, *Men I've Loved Before*

'Love is so much more complicated than I thought it was. I was so dim.'

Steph, *About Last Night*

FINDING THE ONE

Judging A Book By Its Cover

Helena sank back into her couch, balancing a floral china teacup and saucer and two plain biscuits, and took a moment to admire the neat and tidy environment she'd re-established. She loved the children coming home from university for the weekend. She liked to hear their news and see them eat properly; she didn't mind that they brought a huge bag of laundry each. She was their mother and as such would do anything to help them and look after them. That was what mothers were for. Besides, Olivia and Mattie never took her for granted; they were both truly grateful for her attention and concern. They pecked her on the cheek as they showered her with thank yous and 'You're the best, Mum.' Helena knew that at nineteen and twenty-one her offspring were officially adults, but they still seemed very young to her. Life was so tough, stressful and expensive nowadays, much harder than when she and Eddie had started out; the children often appeared to be just as vulnerable as they were on their very first day of school. She encouraged them to come home as regularly as possible. She didn't mind the extra work.

That said, they were incredibly messy. After they returned to their universities, the house always had the appearance of a flustered maiden aunt who had had one too many sherries at a wedding reception: everything was a little askew and nothing made sense. White towels were bruised with smudges of mascara, plates of half-finished food took refuge under Mattie's bed, jars and bottles repelled their lids, bins spat out litter and tables were tattooed with coffee cup rings.

Mrs Cooper, Helena's cleaner, came in every Wednesday for three hours and had been doing so for eighteen years. Helena had decided she could not wait for Wednesday to have calm and order restored in the house, so she'd tidied it herself. For one thing, Mrs Cooper was asthmatic and older than Helena by a generation, and therefore not an especially effective cleaner. Anything beyond light dusting was a stretch. Helena didn't actually need a cleaner, as she was the only one at home nowadays, but she kept Mrs Cooper because she appreciated continuity. She couldn't very well just fire the woman after so many years of devotion (as Eddie had done to Helena). Besides, there were certain things a woman of Helena's standing was supposed to have – a detached property, a cleaner, a window cleaner, a husband who worked in the City. She hadn't been able to hold on to her husband, but she was determined to cling to the rest.

Their divorce had been relatively amicable. Eddie had moved to Hong Kong with his younger, prettier, blonder (sillier!) PA and left Helena with the family home and enough cash to get by. Guilt, she supposed, had motivated him to find his way to a squabble-free arrangement. She didn't miss him any more; he'd been absent long before they divorced. She found she'd been able to fill the gap he left with nothing more than a tasteful flower arrangement.

She sipped her tea and surveyed the now dust-free surfaces, the neatly stacked magazines and the polished floorboards with the same pleasure with which other women ogled Bradley

Cooper. A tap at the front door awoke her from her domestic fantasy.

'Afternoon, Helena.'

Helena sighed quietly. She'd really prefer it if David, the window cleaner, called her Mrs Jackson, but he insisted on being familiar. If ever she tried to call him Mr Simmons (which was the name on his van), he'd make a joke about his dad being retired and insist that she call him Dave; they compromised with David.

'Would you be so good as to refill my bucket?' David asked with a polite smile. He always asked for fresh water, but Helena didn't mind. It was an unequivocal joy to her when the sunlight bounced through her streak-free windows and splattered into her immaculate front room. 'Have you been spring-cleaning?' he asked, craning his neck into the spotless hallway.

David was always cheerful and made pleasant small talk. On cold, blowy days he commented how fresh everything was; on hot days he didn't grumble but said it was lovely weather to be outside in. Eddie had always been dour; he didn't do chat. Not that it was fair to compare the two men. David was a window cleaner and was therefore carefree, with little responsibility. Eddie had an important job with a great deal of stress; of course he was too busy to chat. Or to be kind. He never noticed Helena's polished surfaces.

'Would you like a cold drink? I've some delicious home-made lemonade, though I hasten to add it wasn't made in *this* home. I bought it from a farm at the weekend. The children were here; we had a jaunt out.'

David followed her through to the kitchen. 'How are the kids? Working hard?'

'Fine, I think. The only thing they worry about is me. Olivia suggested I try speed dating! Can you imagine? That suggestion came hot on the heels of suggesting internet dating last time she was home.' Helena rolled her eyes. 'She thinks I'm short of company.'

'Are you?'

'Not at all.'

David had been cleaning Helena's windows for five years. For four of those years they'd barely spoken to one another. Sometimes she'd sit in a room as he cleaned the windows outside that same room and she wouldn't acknowledge him; instead she'd keep her nose buried in her novel. She'd found it a strangely uncomfortable situation. It wasn't that she wanted to be rude; it was more that she didn't really know what to say to him. What could they possibly have in common? Then, about a year ago, David had asked for some clean water and she'd obliged. Naturally, they'd shared a few words. Now they had a cup of tea or a juice together almost every week. Helena was surprised to discover that she found David extremely easy to talk to. He knew all about the trials of her children's exams; he understood her anxiety as to whether she ought to move her once fiercely independent father into an assisted-living flat. How far must a good daughter go? David knew a lot about Helena's life.

She knew nothing of his.

He wore a wedding ring, so she thought any enquiry she might make would seem inappropriate. She also thought it would be inappropriate to admit that yes, sometimes she *was* short of a certain type of company. The company she couldn't get from chatting to her cleaner, or her window cleaner, or even her friends at the book group.

Nervously she searched around for a new topic of conversation. Suddenly David seemed very big and very male standing in her neat and gleaming kitchen. He must have been having the same thought himself; his eyes flicked around the room and then settled – with some relief – on Helena's novel.

'What are you reading?'

'It's the book group's choice.'

'Any good?'

He picked up the book and started to read the blurb on the back. Irrationally, Helena felt embarrassed. She wasn't sure it was the sort of book a window cleaner would enjoy. It was a very deep and complex novel, split into two parts: half set in nineteenth-century India, the other part twenty years in the future.

'I'm enjoying it.'

'Why?'

Helena always had a book on the go, sometimes two. She loved diving into stories and living other people's lives for a short time. She enjoyed being challenged, exploring the world and expanding her vocabulary – all from the comfort of her front room. But whenever anyone asked her why she enjoyed reading, she found it impossible to articulate.

'Oh, it's, erm, unexpected,' she mumbled. 'Fancy a biscuit?'

'I think he sounds interesting?' said Cat, with the cheeky, wink-wink grin that Helena knew so well and dreaded so much.

'Who sounds interesting?' asked Eliza.

'Helena's window cleaner.'

'Oughtn't we to talk about the book?' asked Helena.

It frustrated her that every month the book group followed the same chaotic course. Wine would be poured, nibbles handed around and the chatter and gossip would flow. The book would be forgotten.

'We can't start yet. Not everyone's here,' said Julie. 'We're expecting a new member.'

The worst thing about the gossip, as far as Helena was concerned, was that the others tended to focus only on her situation. They all had partners and were either blissfully happy or horribly miserable in their relationships; it seemed neither condition was as fascinating as her single status. Since Eddie had left her, the book group's *raison d'être* had shifted from discussing analogy, imagery and plot to finding Helena a new man.

Helena was reluctant. It was difficult to imagine meeting anyone new. When asked what she was looking for in a man, she'd say she wanted someone steady, financially secure, diligent.

'Dull, you mean,' objected Cat the first time she heard the list of prosaic expectations.

'I mean someone like Eddie.'

'But Eddie had an affair and left you.' Cat resisted adding that Eddie *was* dull.

'Like Eddie but without the affair,' admitted Helena.

'I think you should try something totally different,' insisted Cat.

Helena had found herself dragged to salsa classes, life drawing classes, and even a bowling club. Cat wanted her to meet someone with hobbies; Eddie had had no interests outside work (he'd even chosen his mistress from the selection offered at the office). Helena had yet to meet a man she liked at any of these places. She wasn't convinced by snaky hips or the 'Do you want to come up and see my etchings?' line. These arty men were unsuitable. Now Cat was becoming fascinated by Helena's window cleaner; it was a terrifying thought. Cat was a force to be reckoned with when she latched on to an idea; she was like a starving dog with a juicy bone. Helena was certain she did not want to date her window cleaner. She had to nip the idea in the bud instantly.

'He's not my type.'

'You don't have a type; there's only ever been Eddie,' said Eliza.

'Window cleaners earn good money nowadays, you know,' added Julie.

Helena blushed. 'It's not the money. I don't need money. It's . . .' She didn't know how to phrase it without sounding snobby. 'I don't think we'd have that much to talk about.'

'But you said you find him easy to talk to. You tell him all about your kids and your dad.'

'Yes, but I'm not sure he'd have any interest in art, or literature, or even politics.'

Cat hooted with laughter. 'He might be a perfect bit of rough.'

'That's what you think I need, is it?' said Helena, trying not to become flustered.

'Who's to say he's rough just because he works with his hands?' demanded Karen. She was trying to make a sensible point, but Cat just shrieked with laughter again and made a joke about the importance of finding a man who was good with his hands. The token male group member, Ian, wriggled uncomfortably in his chair.

The doorbell rang, saving Helena.

'Can I introduce Dave Simmons,' said Julie with a beam.

For a nanosecond Helena didn't recognise David. She knew his face as well as the back of her hand, but seeing him out of context and in smarter clothes startled her. He startled all the other female members of the group too. They sat with their backs straight and chests out, grinning and wide-eyed.

'Take a seat next to Helena,' said Cat, pointing to the free chair. Helena smiled at David, but before they had the chance to tell the rest of the group that they knew one another, Ian seized the moment to talk about the book.

'I don't suppose you've had chance to read it yet, have you, Dave?'

'I just picked it up this week but managed to finish it this morning.'

'Good going. It's chunky, isn't it?'

'Yes, but fascinating.'

'What did you like about it, Dave?' asked Cat.

'I was transported. The descriptions were lyrical. The characters were so complex and believable, even though their dilemmas were very removed from my own experience.'

9

Helena couldn't agree more. She nodded enthusiastically but somehow couldn't find her tongue. For the rest of the evening she listened as David enthused about books. He was familiar with many of the classics and most of the recent prizewinners. He'd read lots of the books she had bought and knew she ought to read but had never got round to. He had an opinion on them all. She was enthralled by each well-observed point he made and mesmerised by his perception and confidence. He was nothing like she'd thought him to be. How had she known him for five years and not known him at all? The extent of her prejudice shamed her. Shivers of terror ran up her spine: she had to find a way of ensuring that none of the others inadvertently exposed her by resuming the conversation about her window cleaner. If he was mentioned, she was sure her snobbery and narrow-mindedness would be uncovered. She waited for a pause in the discussion and an appropriate moment to mention her relationship with David. None came.

Helena remained tense all evening; she wanted to get home. She'd call them all tomorrow and explain the situation. Then she'd leave the group. As wonderful as the book club was, she wouldn't be able to face the members after she confessed that she had a thing for the window cleaner – who she'd previously dismissed. She struggled to find the arm of her coat. Over and over again she jabbed at the sleeve but somehow couldn't twist it the correct way to put it on.

David helped her.

'Thanks.' A blush flared on her neck and crept up to the roots of her hair.

'You were very quiet this evening. I thought you liked the book.'

'I do. It's just that—'

She didn't get a chance to finish the sentence as Cat appeared at their side. Cat lived just five minutes' walk from Julie's and so had seen off almost a bottle of wine. Thus fortified she asked, 'Are you married?'

'Widowed, actually.'

'Oh,' said Helena. 'I'm sorry.'

'Nine years ago now. Look, maybe we could go for a coffee and you can tell me your thoughts on the book without a crowd,' he said.

'Don't waste your time, Dave. You're not her type,' grinned Cat.

Helena froze.

'She has a type?' asked David, with a curious and friendly grin.

Helena thought she might be ill on Julie's hall carpet.

'Yes, she's after a bit of rough. She fancies her window cleaner. You, sir, are far too educated,' joked Cat.

'That's very interesting,' said David. Helena wouldn't meet his eyes but she could feel them boring into her. 'Do you think it's fair to have such preconceptions? Couldn't you give me a chance?'

Helena forced herself to look up. 'You're right. Just because you're well read doesn't necessarily mean you won't know what to do with your hands. I'd love a coffee.'

Bird Of Paradise

Riley and Mason stood side by side, shoulder to shoulder, silently encouraging and supporting, just as they had done on endless past occasions when they'd faced their headmaster or their mothers after being caught in scrapes, as mischievous boys are bound to be; or as teenagers, when Brian-built-like-a-brick shithouse and his gang of morons wanted their lunch money and they'd refused to give it up – a stand neither could have made alone. They'd stood shoulder to shoulder for various team photos, at bars, in ski lifts, before exams and job interviews, and now at the altar.

Riley was taking the plunge.

It was a surprise to everyone that he was marrying first. Mason was the romantic, Riley the cynic – but then Emma had crash-bang-walloped into his life. Emma was pretty, funny and intelligent; Riley was ga-ga. Mason didn't resent that their double act had become a triple act; a best mate shouldn't, couldn't begrudge a pal finding true love.

He wouldn't mind a bit of the same himself.

The bright sunlight slipped through the stained-glass window, making Riley's face look as though a five year old had gone to town with the crayons. Despite the colour, he still looked worse than he had the morning after his stag party. Mason wondered whether grooms ever threw up in the font, through nerves.

'You OK, mate?'

'Fine,' replied Riley, managing a tight nod.

'Don't worry, she'll turn up. She loves weddings; she's not going to miss her own.'

Truthfully, Mason loved weddings almost as much as Emma did, although he'd let wild horses tear him limb from limb before he'd admit it. He loved everything about them, from the intense, heady smell of the lilies to the smart suits and pretty floral dresses that the guests wore. He thought confetti, champagne and even mediocre coronation chicken had an allure. His all-time favourite moment was when the bride stepped through the church door, swathed in petticoats and veil. The congregation always gasped because that moment was one of intense possibility and wonderful optimism. He couldn't help himself: as unfashionable as it was, he was a diehard romantic.

Truly petrified, Riley stared resolutely ahead. Mason glanced over his shoulder and noted that the church was nearly full.

'My God, she's gorgeous,' he murmured. He hadn't intended to blaspheme in church; he hadn't intended to speak out loud, but when he set eyes on the woman in the brown dress, yellow scarf and – wow, that was brave – green shoes, he was knocked momentarily insensible. Her glorious rainbow beauty put him in mind of a fabulous exotic bird of paradise.

'Who is that woman in the brown, yellow and green?' he asked.

'I don't know. I wasn't aware we knew anyone who was colour blind,' replied Riley.

'She's an absolute beauty,' said Mason.

Riley forced himself to sneak a peek at the congregation. He was almost a married man but he could not fail to notice the well-endowed beauty in the brown dress.

'No, no, mate. You mustn't touch her. That's Tabitha, Emma's boss. She eats men like us for breakfast. She's a horror. Emma only invited her because she'd be sacked if she didn't,' he said.

Mason stole a second glance; the bird of paradise was beaming broadly. He was already in love with her enormous smile. 'She doesn't look like the sort of woman who eats men for any meal,' he commented.

'That's your problem, mate, you never believe people have faults. Trust me: she makes the black widow spider look friendly. Keep away.'

Mason didn't have time to think about the bird of paradise again, because the organ announced that Emma, in all her glory, had arrived.

Everyone agreed the wedding was utterly perfect. The ceremony was stunning, hitting the correct note of sober reverence and evident elation. The reception was idyllic: the guests drank champagne on the lawn and basked in the sun. At the sit-down meal, the food and the speeches were sublime and hilarious respectively. Everybody had a sensational time.

Except Mason.

He tried to catch the bird of paradise outside the church but lost her in the crowd. At the reception, he got a fleeting glance of the brown satin of her skirt but he was crushed – she had her arms wrapped around one of the ushers. Riley was right: fast worker. Mason felt a sting of terrible disappointment deep in his gut. He watched the bird of paradise fly from the arms of the usher to the side of a waiter, and then, during the meal, he saw her flirt with *all* the men on her table. He couldn't hear exactly what she was saying or catch her expressions, as she had her back to him, but her actions left little to the imagination. She fed profiteroles (with her mouth!) to the guy to her left throughout Mason's speech; a speech she interrupted at inappropriate times with a low, throaty, drunken laugh. He'd imagined, having clocked

15

her smile in the church, that her laugh would be more joyous – less dirty.

He was a damn fool to have these idealistic views of women.

'Mate, can you scoop up Tabitha and sober her up; she's passed out under the table and we can't cut the wedding cake with her legs sticking out from under it; it will ruin the photos,' said Riley.

'Can't you ask someone else?' grumbled Mason, but he stood up to move the drunken woman; he was the best man after all. As carefully as he could, considering her comatose state, he eased her out from under the table.

My God, she was barely recognisable. She *wasn't* recognisable. This wasn't his exotic bird. Same dress, yes, same scarf and shoes, but even if she had been conscious, he instinctively knew that this woman would not bestow face-splitting smiles. Big boobs, yes, but not a sign of an enormous grin.

Confused, Mason carried the wilting woman towards the loos. She needed water splashed on her face and then she'd need black coffee. He debated for a moment whether to take her into the ladies' or the gents'. Both were riddled with potential embarrassment, but the men's smelt worse and the women's had a powder room; maybe they'd have comfy seats where he could deposit her.

He opened the door and there was Heidi, Emma's second cousin once removed, a woman who also loved weddings, everything from the delicate ballet slippers the bridesmaids wore to the perky buttonholes. Heidi had been determined to love *this* wedding, even though before she'd even settled into her pew, two elderly aunts had asked her if she was seeing anyone special and one old uncle had assured her it was her turn next. She knew the uncle's confidence was misplaced, as her love life was as dry as an AA meeting. Her only consolation had been that a wedding was an excuse to buy a new outfit, and she'd been extremely pleased with hers. She'd blown a silly amount on a chocolate halter-neck dress, boldly teamed with a saffron scarf and emerald shoes, just as the outfit was presented on the mannequin in the window. This morning she'd stood immodestly in front of the mirror and twirled around and around, made giddy by the floaty material.

In the church, she had stared in horror as she noticed (how could she fail to) the woman click-clack her way over the ancient enamel tiles and settle in the pew in front. The woman was tall and tanned, and although Heidi had never seen her before in her life, she was oddly familiar: the two of them were wearing the exact same outfit.

Shocked, Mason and Heidi stared at one another. The exotic bird unable to take her eyes off the unconscious fashion faux pas in Mason's arms; Mason unable to take his eyes off the woman he'd hunted all day.

'What are you doing in here?' he asked.

'Hiding,' said Heidi.

'How long have you been in here?'

'Since the ceremony. I had no alternative, shame really. I love weddings, but you may have noticed, I'm in the exact same outfit as your girlfriend.'

'She isn't my girlfriend,' said Mason quickly. 'Not my type, although she clearly has great dress sense.'

Heidi laughed. It was a joyful, blissful laugh – just the sort Mason had imagined would be the call of a bird of paradise.

The Real Thing

Viv turned the key in the lock and gave the door a sharp kick so that the warped wood shifted. The old-fashioned shop bell chimed as she stepped over the threshold. She bent to sweep up the post (unwanted circulars and bills) and to briefly pet the shop cat, before he darted outside. She took a deep breath and absorbed the unique smell of dust, wood polish and old books, her equivalent of lavender or chamomile. This was her favourite moment of the day. She was all alone in her beloved shop and everything was possible and ahead of her.

Viv had been running Viv's Vintage for six years now. Owning a shop that sold elaborately decorated teacups, wax flowers under glass domes and heavily embroidered tablecloths was not, perhaps, what she'd had in mind when she gained her degree in business studies, but it suited her. She occasionally stumbled across an article about one of her fellow students in the *FT* or even *Time* magazine. They all worked at huge multinational conglomerates and had impressive titles that included the words 'chief' and 'officer'. The titles alone terrified Viv; irrationally, they brought to mind images of an army of people doing the goosestep in heels. If any of her peers had jumped off the corporate ladder, it was to bring up a cluster of beautiful and brilliant children. Viv didn't have beautiful and brilliant children; she didn't even have plain, daft ones. She had a series of confidence-sapping broken relationships, none of which had culminated in marriage, all of which had required her to put her own career on the back burner; she'd moved around the country supporting and rushed around the home cleaning and cooking and caring. After the last break-up, she'd sworn off men, decided it was time to concentrate on herself. She'd assessed what it was, exactly, that she was good at.

Kate, her oldest friend, commented, 'Shopping.'

'That's it? You think that's the sum total of my talents? I can shop?'

'You've a good eye for spotting unusual things, and despite being a bit of a wallflower, you drive a hard bargain. You should turn your hobby of collecting stuff into a career.'

Viv accepted Kate's advice, primarily because she really couldn't think of a better idea. Kate and Viv were an unlikely pairing: chalk and cheese. Kate had always planned to take a year off to travel once she'd graduated, but one year had turned into two, stretched to five, bulged into a decade and more. Now, all these years later, it was accepted that she was of no fixed abode, at least rarely for longer than a year or so. Still, she felt more than adequately compensated because she had meditated outside the Taj Mahal, seen the sunset from the top of Kilimanjaro and flown a helicopter over the Grand Canyon (actually flown it; she was not just a passenger!). Viv envied Kate's ability to carelessly dismiss everyone else's definition of success; it seemed so brave and exciting. Kate didn't own much at all – she rented properties and borrowed, bought and sold furniture as needed. Viv was the opposite: she felt most secure when her fridge and cupboards were bursting. It was lucky that she'd managed to turn her interest in bric-a-brac into a business.

Sometimes Kate brought home something special from her

travels. Viv would buy it and sell it on in the shop, at no profit at all, because she liked to supplement Kate's low income but she didn't like passing the expense on to her loyal customers.

The sun shone through the shop window, reflecting and refracting the light from the various glass ornaments like glitter or a disco ball. Viv knew the shop was most likely to be quiet today because people would rather lie flat on their backs in their gardens and bask, rather than mooch around a shop cluttered with collectibles. Still, she'd catch up on some paperwork. The British summer was invariably fleeting; no one could begrudge the odd sunny day.

'Hello!'

'Kate, what a surprise!' The women threw themselves into an uninhibited affectionate hug. 'When did you get back?'

'This morning.'

'Wonderful! It's so good to see you. What are your plans?'

'I have a couple of options.' Kate always had options, chances and choices. 'I've brought you something.' She reached into her enormous, tatty, cardboard-stiff rucksack. Wasn't there an age when rucksacks simply became undignified, like mini skirts and piercing your belly button? 'Look, a Stetson. Isn't it fabulous? It's a No. 1 Quality; it's over a hundred years old. Look at the wonderful pencil-curl brim, and that "Fray" sweatband was invented and patented by one of Stetson's earliest employees.'

Viv took the battered black felt cowboy hat from Kate. Hats weren't her area of expertise, but she suspected that, whatever Kate had been told, this was not a genuine Stetson. 'What did you pay for it?'

Kate named an astronomical price. Viv gasped. She didn't know how to tell her friend she'd been conned. 'It has a story attached,' Kate continued. 'It belonged to this bad-boy bank robber.'

'Did it now?'

'However, I don't want a penny. Can I just have use of your sofa for a week or two?'

Viv knew that Kate was likely to be on her sofa all summer; she didn't care, she'd have offered anyway, but now she had a graceful way around avoiding declaring the hat worthless.

The women's ebullient chatter was interrupted by a polite cough. Viv, clocking who'd entered, turned pink; the deep blush mottled her soft skin. Kate noticed the man – who was saved from being called ordinary-looking because he had kind eyes and broad shoulders – and realised this must be Reubén Nicholls, who regularly featured in Viv's emails. Reuben was one of Viv's most regular customers; he stopped by twice a week and always bought something. Viv hadn't worked out what his area of interest was. Once he bought a pair of brass binoculars; another time some antique engraved mother-of-pearl Chinese gaming chips, and last week he'd purchased a souvenir biscuit tin from the coronation of HM Queen Elizabeth II. She reported that he always spent ages mooching about the shop but his purchases were often impulsive; if another customer came in, he'd guiltily pick up the nearest thing to hand, a bit like a woman on a diet grabs a chocolate bar at the till.

When Reuben spotted Kate, he turned to leave; stupendously shy, he preferred to have the shop to himself. Viv understood that. Although it was her job to sell her goods, she actually preferred it when the shop was empty and it was just her and her beautiful curiosities. Or her and Reuben.

Kate saw the matter clearly. Not one who was backward at coming forward, she found it frustrating that Viv was so shy about asking for what she wanted. Given the amount of stuttering, and the fact that he was practically backing out of the door, Kate guessed Reuben was no more forthright, and so decided to intervene.

'Come in, come in. You're just in time.' She grabbed his arm.

'In time for what?' Reuben and Viv both looked nervous.

'New stock. Look at this Stetson.' Kate held up the hat as though she was displaying a hard-won sporting trophy. Reuben looked surprisingly interested.

'You know, it's just the sort of thing I've been looking for.'

'You don't want to buy that!' cried Viv, aghast.

'I do. I'll give you eighty pounds for it.'

Viv feared that Reuben was simply making an impetuous gesture because he wanted to get out of the shop as quickly as possible. Sometimes she wondered why he came in at all.

'No. You can't.' She didn't know how to stop him without revealing to Kate that it was a fake.

'Deal,' laughed Kate.

'Where will you wear it?' asked Viv weakly, desperately trying to think of a reason for him not to buy it.

'Well.' Reuben took a deep breath and plunged. 'As luck would have it, there's a country and western night at the Eagle pub this evening. I was thinking of going.'

'We should go too,' said Kate, landing a not-too-subtle nudge in Viv's ribs.

Reuben hesitated, then added, 'Company would be nice.'

'That's really not my thing.'

'What *is* your thing?' Kate muttered, not managing to hide her irritation. She had repeatedly asked Viv to come travelling with her, or at least take a holiday, but Viv had always refused, as she refused anyone who offered to buy her a coffee or take her to the cinema. She used the same excuse every time: 'It's not my thing.'

'We'll be there at seven, latest,' declared Kate.

When Reuben left, Kate turned and beamed at Viv triumphantly; Viv refused to give Kate the satisfaction of talking about what had just happened. What *had* happened? Had Reuben asked her out? No, impossible. So had he asked Kate? That was much

23

more likely. And the hat! She'd just knowingly passed off a fake as a genuine antique. It was unethical. It felt deeply wrong. She couldn't talk about it. Instead she dusted her collection of Wade whimsies. Kate, realising she wasn't going to get any thanks for her efforts, said she'd head off, they could meet later at the Eagle.

Viv felt hot and flustered all day. She didn't want to go to the pub to meet Reuben, especially as he was so obviously keen on Kate, but she knew she had to. She had to return his money at the very least. She locked the shop door, fighting a sense of dread and gloom. Even the warm evening and the sight of old people sitting companionably on the benches and young people in boisterous groups drinking lager didn't cheer her up.

The pub was heaving, a sea of checked shirts, cowboy hats and boots. Viv's heart sank. Through the throng she spotted Kate, already chatting animatedly with Reuben. It was obvious that they were completely smitten with each other because neither of them seemed aware of the fact that was most glaring to Viv: nearly half the men in the bar were wearing the exact same Stetson as the one she'd sold to Reuben.

She'd go over and say hello and tell him she'd come to return the money. That done, she'd slink away and tell herself she hadn't been gently flirting with Reuben for four months; that Kate was welcome to him.

'Here she is! What are you drinking?' Kate asked as Viv approached. 'Look, the barman is wearing a No. 1 Quality too,' she laughed.

'You knew it was a fake?'

'I didn't *know*. I thought the guy on the market might be telling porkie-pies.' Kate shrugged.

'But I thought you'd picked it up in Wyoming.'

'I never actually said that.'

'You took eighty quid for it!'

'Technically *you* did.'

Viv turned to Reuben. 'I am so, so sorry. Look, here's your money. I'll leave you two to it. I'm sorry she sold you a fake. I'm sure she can make it up to you.'

Reuben stared at Viv, then at Kate; he looked confused.

'I wasn't trying to con anyone and *I'm* not the one in a position to make anything up to him, can't you see? You like him. He likes you. You're both shy, I thought I'd help. I didn't know he'd ask you to this but I did know you'd track him down to return the cash and have an actual conversation, instead of behaving like tongue-tied teenagers.'

Reuben took off the hat. Viv thought he might throw it down in protest but instead he placed it carefully on her head. 'It's OK. It's all OK. Your friend's right. She didn't sell me a fake. I've got the real thing.' And with that he gently put his hand on the small of Viv's back and led her towards the bar.

Categorically Not My Type

Lottie walked the few strides from the kitchen to the living room, carefully balancing her mug of strong, sweet tea in one hand and her gossipy magazine in the other. Before her bottom hit the seat, Henry swirled around her legs and leapt up, nearly upsetting the tea.

She put the mug on the side table and flung herself into the comfy armchair. 'Darling, be careful. You don't want to get scalded, do you, you daft cat.'

Henry purred, settled on Lottie's lap and started to rhythmically knit his claws into her jeans. Lottie didn't really mind his enthusiasm for cuddling up; in fact she loved it. It was nice to be wanted! Her best friend, Ellie, said that Henry was a boyfriend replacement; which just showed what Ellie knew about cats *and* men. Lottie had never come across a man who was clean, independent and playful.

She sipped her tea and flicked the pages of her magazine. None of the articles held her attention. Shame, as all she had to do tonight was read the mag, watch her favourite soap and pop something in the microwave. Pretty much the same routine she'd followed every evening for four months, since she split up with her last, not-very-serious boyfriend, Mick. Ellie kept insisting that

Lottie ought to get out and meet new people (she meant a new man), but where did people meet people nowadays? Not in bars or clubs, that was for certain. Throughout her early twenties Lottie was always dashing about – clubbing, shopping, working – just having so much fun that meeting anyone, let alone the One, hadn't seemed a priority.

In her late twenties she found dinner parties became the new nightclubs. She tended to know the people she was invited to dine with, cosy couples who always invited a 'spare' man for her to look over. She found it mortifying and couldn't concentrate on these guys that also seemed embarrassed and considering themselves tantamount to sacrificial offerings.

More recently she'd tried online dating but men lied about their hobbies (they never had as many as they claimed) and their weight (they always had more than they claimed). Ellie said the problem was that Lottie was too picky. Lottie retorted that there was nothing wrong with having standards.

'Yours are Olympic standards. You don't give anyone a chance.'

Henry had been there for Lottie throughout all these trials and tribulations. She had adopted him on her twenty-third birthday and he'd been loyally by her side when internet dating and speed dating proved to be fruitless and pointless respectively. That was why the thing with Mick was doomed: Lottie discovered that he was allergic to cat fur. Men came and went. Henry was a permanent fixture.

The doorbell rang and a loud and constant barking started up.

'Oh bother. It's Jake from downstairs again,' muttered Lottie. 'You stay here, sweetheart, and I'll get rid of him.'

Jake was a nice enough guy. Quite good-looking, actually. Lovely green eyes and a kind smile; large hands, which Lottie had a thing for, but still, she had no time for him. It was his irritating, noisy dog that she objected to. Jake had started calling by Lottie's relatively frequently. He'd take in her deliveries (didn't he have a job?), or if he was off to the shops he'd ask if she needed anything (did she look like a pensioner?). Problem was, every time he stopped by, he had his noisy mutt with him. Poor Henry nearly climbed the walls with fright.

'Hi, Lottie. Sit still, Tilly,' said Jake, trying (and failing) to restrain his dog's exuberance. Lottie sighed quietly as a glob of Tilly's saliva hit her shoe. 'Lottie, I'm going to get straight to the point. Erm. Well. Straight to it after three months of visiting you on tenuous excuses. Would you like to come out for a drink with me sometime? Or maybe a movie?'

What an uncomfortable situation! Lottie didn't want to be rude, but what could they possibly have in common? He was a dog lover. She was a cat lover. The relationship was a non-starter. Tilly panted, yelped and growled whilst Jake waited for his answer. For once Lottie didn't mind the noise; at least it filled the silence.

'No thanks,' she muttered, and then quickly closed the door, as though she was disposing of an uninvited salesman.

She hurried back to Henry. Cats were such sensitive souls. Tilly's barking had clearly upset him more than Lottie could have imagined. Henry would not come near her for the rest of the evening and sulked in the kitchen.

Jake stopped calling. Oddly, Lottie missed him. It wasn't just that she had to go to the post office depot to pick up her parcels; she missed his beam and his easy chatter. She hadn't been aware that she was so used to him. Plus, Henry seemed to be out of sorts too. Nothing specific; just lacklustre, off his food and not playful.

One day Lottie came home from work early with the intention of taking Henry to the vet to be checked over if he hadn't perked up. She was stunned to find him chasing a butterfly in Jake's front garden, with Tilly! Cat and dog were cavorting happily together (although the butterfly probably wasn't having much fun). Jake was sitting on the front doorstep watching them.

'What's going on?' demanded Lottie.

'Oh, erm, hi.' Jake looked embarrassed. 'Nothing new. We always spend our lunch hour like this. Weather permitting. It's one of the benefits of working from home.'

Lottie pointed at Henry and Tilly. 'Doesn't the expression "fight like cat and dog" mean anything to those two?'

'Actually, *they* are the best of friends.' Jake's heavy emphasis did not go unnoticed. Now it was Lottie's turn to be embarrassed. 'I guess they don't have any preconceptions or rules about that kind of thing.'

'I guess not,' agreed Lottie.

'In fact, when Tilly isn't with Henry, she pines for him.' So Henry wasn't ill! 'And that's why she's always so boisterous when we drop by yours.' And why Henry became wild; it was excitement, not fear. How could Lottie have failed to see that? She risked grinning at Jake.

'You know, cats are very intelligent creatures. Everyone can learn a thing or two from them,' she said shyly.

'And dogs are very loyal, also an admirable quality,' added Jake. 'So, about that drink . . .'

Chemistry

'It's great to see everyone enjoying the hot weather, isn't it?' says Carrie, as we rush through St James's Park, past barefooted babies kicking off their buggy blankets, and oldies in deckchairs enjoying an ice cream and the music provided by the buskers.

'Suppose,' I mutter, only just avoiding tripping over an embracing couple sprawled on the grass.

'Sorry,' they say in unison, eyes locked on each other.

I glower, but don't reply, just hurry on. 'To be honest, I think the Brits suit winter more than summer,' I comment.

'What?'

'We haven't quite got that *je ne sais quoi* to carry off all this . . .' I look around me, ostensibly to search for the right word, but I find I'm faced with nothing other than happy couples. Couples with their limbs draped over one another, kissing, laughing and chatting. Couples tossing Frisbees and picnicking as though they are filming a montage scene for a rom-com. 'All this indulgence and merriment,' I say bitterly. Carrie laughs, but I'm not joking. 'A week of hot weather and we lose the plot,' I grumble.

'How so?'

I grab my friend's arm and try to encourage her to pick up her pace; the hot weather encourages ambling, which I simply haven't got time for, and we're going to be late. As we dash for the tube, I explain, 'Summer comes and women suddenly start wearing gaudy, ill-fitting, inappropriate clothes, like boob tubes and ra-ra skirts, which are only acceptable if you haven't yet had your eighth birthday party or you're a supermodel.' Carrie stares at me in bewilderment, but I'm on a roll. 'Men confuse which item of clothing belongs where, so you get handkerchiefs on heads, socks under sandals and an entire removal of T-shirts, which is *not* recommended unless you're as buff as Jamie Dornan. It's horrible.'

'Why are you in such a mood?' demands Carrie, with the brutal honesty that is the sole reserve of my best friend.

I sigh dramatically. How can I explain it? I don't mind being single quite so much in the winter – I like cosying up in front of the TV with a baggy jumper to keep me warm and a box of chocs to answer all my emotional needs – but somehow during the summer I feel more exposed. My single status seems so blatant when the sunshine draws out a seemingly endless trail of happy, laughing couples. I don't answer Carrie's question directly but say, 'Where do people meet people nowadays?'

This is not the first time I've asked Carrie this particular question. She's sympathetic because her love life is also as dry as the Gobi Desert but she doesn't have the answers. It must be some sort of addiction that we frequently feel the need to restate the hopelessness of our situation. The fact that we're now sitting in a hot, stuffed commuter train, where people can eavesdrop, doesn't deter us.

'Not in bars or clubs, that's for certain,' Carrie replies. Throughout my early twenties I waited for Cupid to aim true, but he kept missing, perhaps because I was always sweaty from dancing with wild abandon (his arrows just slipped off me). It didn't matter then. Nothing did.

'Nor at dinners thrown by well-meaning matchmaking friends,' I add.

The smug marrieds tried their best; they generously opened their address books but those sources were drained by the time we reached our late twenties. Contacts were dipped into so thoroughly that there were times when I felt there was a danger of drowning in a sea of seemingly keen guys. Sadly, they were all quickly exposed as ruthless players who wanted nothing more than short and shallow affairs. Then, the weirdest thing happened to these callous Casanovas: as they blew out thirty candles on their birthday cakes, they each grabbed the nearest woman and *proposed*. I was always in the other room and was never grabbed.

'Not through personal ads either,' groans Carrie. Because men lie about their age and height and fail to mention wigs and wives until two dreary courses have been endured.

'Internet dating lacks chemistry, you know, the va va voom, plus there's no mystery there,' I say. My last four dates were the result of Tinder but by the time I met those guys, I already knew so much about them – from favourite colours to childhood illnesses – that we struggled for conversation.

'Maybe this speed dating will work,' says Carrie, making an effort to appear optimistic.

'Atchoo.' My sneeze erupts into the packed carriage. I feel the unsympathetic shudder of hot commuters; I want to explain it is hay fever, not the bubonic plague, and that it's not contagious.

'Bless you.'

Stunned by this level of human interface on a tube, I turn to see who is blessing me. Astoundingly, the comment came from a cute-looking thirty-something man. I wonder if I ought to explain commuter law to him. He must be a tourist or else he wouldn't speak.

Suited and booted, clean-shaven, clean-cut, the bless-you man is undeniably handsome. I spend the rest of the four-minute journey sneaking covert glances at him and fantasising about us meeting somewhere other than a train. Somewhere I could strike up a conversation, like people used to. But then he's probably married, or gay. Straight, single men, with their own teeth, are an endangered species. Fact.

Speed dating turns out to be everything I feared it would be. During the day I efficiently manage a large and dynamic sales team who flog fitted kitchens. This is a position I earned after years of cold-calling the unwilling at teatime. People say I could sell snow to Eskimos, but trying to sell my 'quintessential spirit' (as the event organiser suggested) in four minutes flat, whilst balding guys stare down my cleavage, is a trial I'm not equal to.

'Let's go for a drink,' suggests Carrie wearily.

We barely bother to scan the bar; scoping for talent is something the hopeful do, so I'm amazed when Carrie nudges me and says, 'Weird coincidence. Look, there in the corner. Isn't that the guy from the train who blessed you?'

So she noticed him too. I wonder if she also projected as far as birthing his second child before we reached Covent Garden? I start to feel something in my stomach. I can't say it's excitement – that would be too robust a description – but certainly something. Possibility? I can't help but think that maybe people *do* meet in bars and maybe there *is* such a thing as fate. Two sightings in one night, in a city of over eight million inhabitants, must mean something.

'Don't look, he's coming over,' hisses Carrie.

We hastily turn away and laugh loudly to give the impression that we're the wittiest women in town. The bless-you man isn't fooled. He walks straight past and into the loos. My imaginary children spontaneously combust.

'Let's go home. I've taken all the disappointment I can bear for one evening,' I mutter.

We ooze gloom as we down our drinks, gather up our bags and head for the door.

'Excuse me, you've forgotten these.' I turn; the bless-you man is holding out my sunglasses.

'Oh, thanks.' I take them from him and our fingers touch for the briefest of moments. *Zap*: it feels like I've been scalded.

He smiles. It's a good smile; it reaches right into his eyes. 'Do I know you? Your face is familiar,' he says.

'Erm, actually, I was on the same tube as you earlier. I sneezed, you blessed me.'

He shakes his head dismissively. 'No, that's not it. I was reading. I don't even remember saying bless you – I just say it automatic- ally – but I do know your face.'

He chews his thumbnail for a moment. It's a long moment. I want to fill it with something fun and flirtatious, but I'm suddenly incapable. I try to remember my four-minute speed-date pitch, but that too escapes me, which – thinking about it – might be a good thing.

'Funny that we were on the same tube,' he mumbles. 'Even if I can't, erm . . .'

'Remember me?'

He looks embarrassed. 'Yeah, but what a coincidence, hey?' He rakes his hand through his hair and adds shyly, 'Some might call it fate, and I *do* know you from somewhere.' Sitting alongside the embarrassment, there is an obscure but irrefutable tension between us that I just about remember. Chemistry.

I attempt a joke. 'Can't possibly be fate, that's been replaced by internet dating profiles.'

'That's where I know you from! I've read your profile online,' he says loudly.

I want to gag him. I don't want people thinking I'm the sort of woman who is so desperate for a date that I advertise myself online, even if it's true and even if everyone does it. Another thought occurs to me.

'You never got in contact.' I'm outraged. He shrugs uncom- fortably. 'Why? Didn't you like my photo?'

'You're striking,' he says simply, which goes some way to

mollifying my outrage. I can see out of the corner of my eye that Carrie is giggling. He shakes his head in bewilderment, 'Of all the bars in all the wor—'

'So why didn't you get in contact?' I interrupt his quote from my all-time-favourite movie.

'You said you liked plonk, and I'm a wine snob. Plus you said you'd never look at anyone who watched action movies, and I love them,' he explains with a shrug.

'How intolerant.'

'Aren't we.' He grins. We fall silent for a moment. I can practically bite the tension.

'You just quoted—'

'*Casablanca*. Yes. I said I liked action movies, but not exclusively.' A man who likes black-and-white romances *and* action movies: how interesting. He's quite a mystery. 'So, do you fancy a drink?' he asks.

The chemical reaction is going nuclear. 'Yeah, you can choose the wine, but I'm still picking the movie.'

Adele Shares . . .

My Holiday Playlist

I think music is a fabulous and vital part of the poolside experience. A song, like a book, can transport you to another place or root you in the moment. Holiday music needs to cover every mood whether that's the relaxed vibe as you're tanning or the excited anticipation as you get ready for a night out. This is what I'm listening to this summer. Don't judge!

1. 'Lush Life', Zara Larsson

2. 'Sing', Ed Sheeran

3. 'Summer Wind', Frank Sinatra

4. 'Feel', Robbie Williams

5. 'Your Song', Ewan McGregor

6. 'Summer', Calvin Harris

7. 'Praise You', Fatboy Slim

8. 'Better Together', Jack Johnson

9. 'Only Love', Ben Howard

10. 'Where Do I Begin', Shirley Bassey (Away Team Mix)

11. 'Perfect Day', Lou Reed

12. 'That Man', Caro Emerald

13. 'The Girl from Ipanema', Frank Sinatra

14. 'Under The Bridge', Red Hot Chili Peppers

15. 'Changes', David Bowie

Let me know what's on your playlist!
@adeleparks #LoveIsAJourney

LOVE IS COMPLICATED

Learning By Heart

Tuesday 12 September
Terrible morning, full of silence. Spend most of it talking to self. But then, arguably, I've spent most of summer holiday talking to self too: Libby (twelve going on twenty) and Oli (ten, male and therefore unlikely to develop past this mental age) ignore nearly everything I say anyway. Odd, I've spent the last six weeks begging for hush and moments of calm, but now the silence of an empty house is deafening.

Kids showed heartbreaking independence today by insisting that I didn't walk them to school gates. Oli pointed out that his school is only up the road, not even as far as the corner shop – where I regularly send him to buy milk if we run out. Libby called the idea that I walk her to the comp gates 'totally gross, social humiliation unrecoverable'. I feel redundant.

Call Imogen, my big sister (as I always do in moments of emotional frailty). Major mistake (as it always is), as she's not sympathetic, simply scarily practical and efficient, pointing out that if I don't have to walk the kids to and from school, I can do more hours at Buns and Butties; the extra cash will be handy.

Very true. Very depressing.

Buns and Butties is the baker's where I've been gainfully

employed since my divorce two years ago. It's not a bad little job. I only get a smidgen above the minimum wage, but Bob-the-boss is flexible on hours and understands about bringing up kids alone (his mother did it and his sister is doing it; who'd have thought I'd ever be so fashionable?). Bob and Sue haven't got kids and they are a bit long in the tooth to bother now. I'm not sure if they ever wanted any. It's not the sort of thing I can ask, though Libby could. She's of that generation where nothing is sacred.

The other day she asked me if I've had 'sexual relations' with Mark yet. They'd had 'the talk' at school and she'd seen an opportunity to embarrass and confuse me with role reversal. Her motivation became clear when her next question (fired at rapid speed) was 'Can I have my belly button pierced?' In an attempt to turn the spotlight away from my relationship, I said I'd think about the piercing. This after nine consecutive months of vetoing the idea!

For the record, Mark and I are having sex. Thank you. At forty-two, with two kids and a decree absolute under my belt, I am officially not-so-young, not-so-free and not-so-single. I'm also not-so-comfortable discussing my sex life with my daughter (or my mother, come to that). I'm not modern enough to deal with it. Let's just say I'm not where I expected to be.

I should have been married to Graham for sixteen years now. I thought that by the time I reached my age, my biggest dilemma would be whether I should use sew-on or iron-on labels to name my kids' school uniforms. Instead, I find that I have genuine concern as to how I should address the man in my life. 'Husband' was so charmingly clear-cut. But Mark is not my husband. He's a man who came round to give me an estimate for converting the loft over a year ago and slowly but surely turned into . . . well, what?

The term 'boyfriend' belongs with training bras and ideas about marrying Rob Lowe.

My mother calls Mark my toy boy, and every time she says it she nudges me and winks. At moments like those I sympathise with my kids: parents never stop having the power to humiliate you. Admittedly, technically Mark *is* a toy boy, as he's six years younger than me. But he isn't in it for the money (I have none; my idea of a sound investment is buying two lottery tickets) and he doesn't have long blond hair or a six-pack. He's receding and cuddly.

Imogen thinks I should openly and frequently refer to him as my partner. 'To claim territory. It's a competitive world and he's a catch.' Even my kids agree with her. Single, I'm a responsibility; they don't want to have to amuse me in my old age (Oli told me). But 'partner' puts me in mind of cowboys ('Howdy, partner').

John, my younger, commitment-phobic brother (thirty-nine, longest relationship five months), says I should call Mark my 'dude', which is proof that he lives on a different planet to anyone else I know. For reasons unclear, he felt compelled to add that I was lucky that anyone took me up at my age. Thanks for that.

How come everyone else seems to have the confidence to label my relationship. Where did my voice go?

Only Mark doesn't seem to care what I call him, as long as I do keep calling him. Which is sweet, I suppose. But then men *are* sweet at the beginning, aren't they? But like cream cakes in a shop window, they go off.

Thinking of which, I should call Bob-the-boss about extra hours.

Tuesday 19 September

Graham, my ex, pays me an unexpected visit whilst the kids are at school.

'What do you want?'

He asks for a cup of tea but I know there is a bigger agenda. He dips his digestive (I gave him a chipped mug – such pettiness helps me) and pushes a brochure towards me.

I'm immediately suspicious. The last time he pushed papers in my direction it was a decree absolute that needed my cross.

'What is it?' I ask sulkily. I've noticed that I often behave like a teenager whenever I'm around my parents; I'm not that mature, confident or graceful when I'm with my ex.

'A prospectus for local night classes. There's all sorts: vocational, recreational, part-time degrees. You could do with a new challenge.'

'You don't think bringing up two kids on my own is challenge enough?'

'Julia learnt all she knows from an evening class on textiles.'

When he says Julia, he means the big-breasted usurper. I know she studied textiles at some poxy night class; he's told me of this achievement four hundred times, conservative guess. It's true that her talents were honed during the evening, and that cotton sheets and silky duvets featured; his infidelity is evidence.

It's annoying that in the fourteen years Graham and I were married, he struggled along as a middle manager at Carpet Wearight, bringing in an adequate but not stupendous salary. We had a nice semi, a fortnight in France every year, and the kids wore 'must have' branded trainers. A nice enough, normal enough life.

Within months of leaving me, he packed in his job and set up an interior design company with the Usurper. I admire his cheek. I mean, the man knows about carpets but that's it; he's never so much as held a paintbrush (or a loo brush or a dust pan and brush come to that) yet suddenly he's advising the population of Leicestershire on mohair cushions and ambient lighting.

Irritatingly, their business has gone from strength to strength – last year they bought a five-bedroom detached and went on three holidays. Me and the kids went to my mum and dad's place in the Costa del Sol. It was fine. You know. Sunny enough. Fine.

Thinking of Graham's cornucopia makes me seethe. I snatch

the digestive out of his hand and tell him to leave. He does, but not before telling me that my curtains are dated and offering a deal on new fabric. I only just resist beating him to death with the remote control.

The kids get home from school, spot the prospectus and declare their father's idea a good one. I spend a fair amount of my time persuading them that education is the key to a successful, happy future and I really believe it to be so (unlike when I'm telling Libby that the boys in her class will respect her individuality if she doesn't wear a padded bra and lip gloss). However, I am disconcerted when they play back my own arguments.

'An underexercised brain is a crime, you said so,' says Oli self-righteously. Did I?

'You should do a course in accountancy, Mum. Accountants are always minted. Every girl needs to be self-sufficient. You can't rely on anyone, least of all men, to pay the bills,' adds Libby. I can believe I said that.

'But I like my job. I don't want to retrain.'

'What do you like about it?' asks Oli.

'I enjoy chatting to the customers, and whilst the checked overall isn't high fashion, it hides my bumps and lumps and doesn't need ironing – which is a godsend, because you cannot imagine how many times I smear or slop in a working day.'

The children stare at me as though I have a large L for loser hovering above my head.

I call Imogen. 'Why the sudden interest in my career, do you think?'

'They're probably embarrassed by what you do.' This is more likely to be *her* viewpoint.

Imogen must talk to Mum, because Mum telephones and suggests I do a course in flower arranging. Crossly, I point out that my life isn't that of a Jane Austen heroine.

Mark pops by to look at the leaky tap in the bathroom. After a minute, miraculously, the insane-making drip-drip ceases.

'I should do a course in DIY,' I joke.

'Good idea,' says Mark, and don't ask me how, but I find myself looking for a pen that hasn't dried up to gunky mess and signing on the dotted line.

Tuesday 26 September

I have blind fear at the thought of embarking on the DIY course (my normal tool of choice being a corkscrew), and I'm dreading actually finding the college. Driving or catching a bus to somewhere unfamiliar sends me into a panic. Imogen thinks it's the start of agoraphobia and recommends that I face my fear. My biggest fear is contradicting my big sis and feeling the onslaught of her inevitable wrath, though obviously I don't tell her this. I ask if she can give me a lift. She can't, but Mark says he will.

I make tea for the kids and arrange for John to sit with them. Libby, outraged, points out that she's thirteen next week and considerably more mature than her uncle. As she says this, John is rolling on the floor, battling with Oli for the TV remote; they can't agree on which violent cartoon to watch. I concede Libby's point and tell her to make sure Uncle John cleans his teeth before he goes to bed.

I snap at Mark twice as I'm sure he's going the wrong way and will hit teatime traffic. He assures me maps are unnecessary and the thirty-five-minute buffer is more than generous. We get to the college in ten minutes and so kill time drinking bitter coffee from a vending machine. Mark leaves me at the classroom door with a casual nod, as though he'll see me in a couple of hours. He does not acknowledge that in reality he has just offered me up as a sacrificial DIY virgin on the altar of Black & Decker.

The tutor arrives and demands we introduce ourselves. I struggle to remember who I am and why I'm here. Someone makes a joke about signing up for DIY, not philosophy. Tutor shoots class clown a silencing stare. I'm relieved; I'm hoping for minimum chat and interaction. No point in striking up conversation as it will inevitably lead to exposure as nut-and-bolt novice plus divorcee. Conclusions will be drawn that I'm only attending this class because I no longer have a man in my life to hang pictures. Not absolutely accurate; I do have Mark, I suppose. But for how long? Not forever, obviously; there's no such thing.

I sometimes wonder why Mark is with me. I'm no Liz Hurley. I'm not much like Nigella Lawson or Carol Vorderman either. Thinking of media celebrities, I've more in common with Lassie: bit of an old dog in need of a haircut, but my bark is worse than my bite.

I try to put Mark out of my mind. Thinking of him makes me nervous. If I was younger, I'd say that thinking of him gives me butterflies, but I'm old enough now to identify the icy grasp of terror.

I glance around the room and size up my classmates, twice meeting the eye of fellow pupils who are doing exactly the same. Happy to note that the class is full of women. Some are pretty young things who appear to be accepting that knights in shining armour are thin on the ground and are striking out for independence; others are ladies in their forties who, like me, have probably been shoved down the road of self-reliance.

Manage to grasp the difference between screws and nails and can identify a surprising number of tools. Begin to feel a small amount of excitement at the prospect of being able to put up a curtain pole without having to call Dad.

At coffee break a smiley woman tells me that custard creams are her favourite biscuits. I can't believe this is true in an age when Hobnobs and other chocolate biscuits are abundant, so recognise that she is just trying to make conversation. I give her my custard cream and ask her if she has any kids. I note that she looks just like me (size fourteen, big hips, no boobs) but she has earrings, lip gloss and a decent haircut, therefore like me but much better. Wonder if I should visit the hairdresser. For the past ten years I've let Mum snip away at my dead ends.

Woman who is me-but-better turns out to be cheery divorcee. Assures me she is 'well shot of him' and says I must understand. I haven't considered possibility that being without Graham is a perk, but faced with direct question feel hard pushed to deny it. Gill gives me the number of her hairdresser and then makes cheeky comments about 'total hunk' who is loitering in the corridor. I turn and am surprised and pleased to discover she is talking about Mark, who tells me he is 'standing by. Just in case.'

Gill winks at me and, as we file back into classroom, whispers, 'Lucky cow.'

Tuesday 3 October

Libby is officially a teenager. She's been training for the role for eight years, sulks, door-slamming and inappropriate attire being her way of life; still, the occasion is monumental.

She's delighted with the earrings, smellies and clothes I've bought her but tells me that her father has promised her an Xbox 360 and new games. I have no clue what this is, other than expensive. Cross with him for being able to outdo me, yet pleased Libby is going to profit. Oli sweetly hands over a book token (that I bought).

Libby spends longer than forever in the bathroom and emerges looking like she's planning to film an MTV pop vid. I tell her that she can't wear eyeliner, rouge and eyeshadow, even if it is her birthday. She says I'm 'totally decayed' calling blusher 'rouge' but flounces into the bathroom to scrub it off.

Kids go to school and I go to Buns and Butties; business is slow, which gives me time to pick out cream cakes for tea. This weekend I'm taking Libby's friends bowling and tonight we're having a family tea, which will be a total horror since I invited the entire clan. Disastrously and unexpectedly all accepted and John is also bringing a date, which means twelve to feed and seat. Matters made considerably worse when Libby asked if she could invite her dad. Had to say yes, even if he did ruin my life. Graham insisting on bringing Usurper and his parents. I am gutless wonder and whilst I rehearse (several thousand times) why this is not acceptable, I find myself saying, 'The more the merrier.'

Presence of Usurper dramatically affects the catering arrangements; it is no longer adequate to pass round plates of sausage rolls. Go to Marks & Spencer and buy their fabulous packs of bite-size delicacies; nip to Argos and buy new tea set (two of them) because we don't own enough matching plates; panic as I pass the newsagent and impulse-purchase bumper pack of streamers and balloons. So far Libby's coming-of-teenage party has cost about the same as my wedding reception. I'll have to sell my kidney to pay for her twenty-first.

Mum and Dad arrive first. They loiter in my small hallway, mumbling something about seats being for guests. No logic to this at all. I crossly tell them they are cluttering up the place and demand they sit down. John and his latest squeeze arrive. It is rarely worth my while committing his ladies' names to memory. Like all the rest, she appears pleasant, gullible and hopeful. I give her a week; ten days at tops. He gives Libby a bottle of sparkly wine. She shouts, 'Wicked!' and I shout, 'No way!' and quickly take it off her.

Imogen and family turn up with big noise and big present. Can't hang about to watch Libby devour paper and discover treasure as Graham and add-ons arrive. Usurper looks sensational – self-absorption and a heavily exercised credit card have paid off. I regret my own lack of lipstick; I'm still red and sweaty from blowing up forty balloons.

Kids disappear to bedroom leaving adults with mortifying

silence. Everyone other than Graham seems to be aware that twenty-first-century approach to divorce (all one big happy family) is actually quite difficult to manage. Old approach (stoning adulterer or at least blanking them) would suit me fine. My out-laws regularly slag off Usurper to me and no doubt do the same about me to her, so all of us in one room is tricky. My mother shoots Graham's mother evils as she hasn't forgiven her for going to Usurper's wedding. Imogen talks loudly about the dangers of cosmetic surgery and stares meaningfully at Usurper's breasts. The men stumble through a conversation about football fixtures, but arguably this would be their subject of choice with best mates; it might be that they are, after all, oblivious to disastrous social occasions. I offer Graham a beer. Usurper says he never drinks cans (a lie). I offer her wine – she makes a crack about Blue Nun. Neither touches my spread; they are going on to 'a really good restaurant' later.

Hands on clock appear to be going backwards. Bell rings and I'm surprised to see Mark. Forgotten I'd invited him. Libby and Oli charge down the stairs, delighted to see him. Mark marches into front room with crate of expensive bottled beer and four bottles of champagne.

'I know Libby can't actually enjoy this, but we'll toast her and she can keep the cork.' He winks at Libby and passes her an envelope. 'This is for you to enjoy, though.'

'Tickets to the Ed Sheeran gig!' She squeals and hugs him. 'That is just the coolest. Thank you!'

I stare at Mark, unable to hide from the fact that his arrival has signalled 'party'. Mention as much to Imogen, who shrugs and comments, 'It always does. Haven't you noticed?'

Tuesday 10 October

Libby is a teenager and I'm menopausal; it's official. All week I've been feeling flushed and tired and now I'm late. Want to ring Imogen and ask if she's suffered the early onslaught of menopause too but can't bring myself to do so – too embarrassing. We've never, ever discussed anything like that. We've each gone through two pregnancies but have maintained the illusion that we have the physical make-up of a Barbie doll (at least 'down there'; sadly, neither of us is blessed with Barbie-like pert boobs or pinched waist). Instead, I call Vicky, who I've been best mates with since I was twelve; we've had every conversation of that sort.

'What makes you think you're menopausal?'

'I went on the web and looked up the symptoms. I have about thirty of the possible thirty-five, and the ones I don't have but should expect are even worse!' I want to cry.

'List,' demands Vicky.

'Hot flushes, trouble sleeping and night sweats.'

'That's probably just because the totally gorgeous Mark has taken to staying over at your place on a regular-ish basis. You've forgotten how sweaty it is sleeping with someone else in the bed.'

'You paint such a romantic picture.' I take a glance at the list of symptoms. I printed them off. 'Irregular heartbeat.'

'I'd put that down to Mark too. His smile makes my heart flutter.'

'Mood swings, sudden tears.'

'Is that a warning?'

'Irritability,' I say with some exasperation. Why can't she take this seriously?

'You've always been a nag.'

I skip over the next two symptoms. One is loss of libido, which I'm not actually experiencing; the next has to do with my front bottom and I can't bring myself to say the relevant words over the phone. Face to face and a glass of wine in hand would be different.

I read on. 'Crashing fatigue, anxiety, feelings of dread, apprehension and doom. Difficulty concentrating, disturbing memory lapses.'

'Robyn, I've known you since forever; this isn't the menopause, this is your personality.'

Possibly.

As Vicky is determined to deny the seriousness of my condition, I decide to shut up. I don't mention the sore boobs or mucked-up cycle. I'll pop to Boots and see if there are any vitamins that can help.

'How are things with you?' I ask out of manners.

'Your brother rang me and asked me for a date.'

'What? I hope you told him where to get off. John's a faithless multiple-timing rat. I wouldn't wish him on my worst enemy, let alone my best friend. He's a selfish, lazy commitment-phobe and yet women just melt. I don't get it.'

'It's his smile.'

'Really? I'd say he smirks. Still, well done you for telling him to hop it.'

'I said yes, actually.'

'Oh.'

Vicky is single. She never married and has no kids. She's had a number of long-term relationships, a couple of which even got to the stage of them living together, but either she or the fella always got cold feet. The up side is that because she hasn't been worn down by constant concerns about SATs, hearing tests, swimming lessons and other maternal business, she looks about ten years younger than I do and has a decent job as a manager at Next. The bad news is she still secretly hankers after 'the One', even though she's witnessed many of her friends arguing with their 'One' over who gets the furniture. No one ever learns from anyone else's mistakes; few of us learn from our own.

'He said that you gave him my number.'

'Well, he's lying.' First of many, no doubt. 'He must have nosed through my address book whilst he was babysitting when I was at my night class.'

'He's taking me to that new Italian in town.'

'Order something expensive.'

Over the years John has dated a number of my friends and without exception it has ended in disaster. My friends never want to acknowledge their own gullibility or his immaturity so, oddly, I get the blame. I'm not looking forward to yet another repeat scenario. Vicky senses my disapproval and becomes defensive.

'You need to learn to trust again. Your problem is you can no longer see opportunity, or goodness, or even possibility *anywhere*.'

'That's not true.'

'Yes it is. Look at the way you treat Mark.'

'I don't treat Mark badly.'

'You hardly notice he's there, Robyn! You spend hours agonising over symptoms for a condition you don't have and no time at all revelling in new love.' What is she talking about? 'And one more thing. You better buy a pregnancy test. Just in case.'

With that she hangs up.

Tuesday 17 October

Bob-the-boss and his missus have gone on holiday. I'm responsible for running Buns and Butties. I can hardly believe that Bob has entrusted me with this position, and from the nervous look on his face when he dropped off the keys, he can't either.

Can't imagine it's *that* tricky. I reassure myself that Bet (who's worked at B&B since before I was a twinkle in my father's eye) is coming in every day. Her arthritis means she won't be much help with serving or skivying, but she's great at terrifying customers into impulse purchases.

This isn't a good time for extra responsibility. I'm in the middle of a serious 'Can we get a puppy for Christmas?' campaign from Oli. He knows dogs are for life – he said that was their appeal, and then looked mournfully at the picture of his father that he keeps on his bedside table. He's probably playing me for a fool with emotional blackmail stuff, but I don't think I'm strong enough to continue to turn down his plea. What if he does need a dog to offer security and I dismiss the request as a scam? I'm thinking Labrador. I'll lose weight walking it. I've no illusions that Oli will be responsible for its exercise, despite his promises. I wasn't born yesterday.

Also, I'm battling with the indignity of early menopause (and the misery of unsympathetic friends), the homework from my DIY course piling up, my best friend dating my feckless brother and then . . . Mark.

Vicky thinks I take him for granted. It's not that I'm complacent – the opposite! I don't want to start to depend on him. OK, at the moment he's always around, buying me chocolate, ensuring that Oli's using the internet for homework, making Libby laugh (often a superhuman feat), but how long for? Maybe I am keeping him at arm's length, but just because he's never done anything to hurt me *yet* doesn't mean he's not going to, does it? Look at Graham.

Actually, Graham's not a good comparison. Hand on heart he'd never have got a Husband of the Year award. He wasn't dreadful but he was never attentive or caring like Mark.

I think about Mark as I check deliveries, clean ovens and put out stock. Libby comes into the shop at lunchtime with her spotty mates. I insist they all eat a pasty and an apple (which I brought from home) before I let them loose on doughnuts. Libby rolls her eyes and says I'm 'pure morty' (as in mortifying, I assume), but I don't care. I pull her to one side.

'Would you say I'm nice to Mark?'

For once, Libby doesn't feel the need to pretend she doesn't understand me.

'Does *he* say you are nice to him?'

'I've never asked him.'

'Duh.' She stares at me in the way I stare at her when I get her school report: vaguely disappointed and frustrated. The phrase 'could try harder' comes to mind. 'You're not awful to him, s'pose.' She's looking at her feet. This conversation is costing her. 'But you don't seem *into* him. Like, when's his birthday?'

'Erm, late February.' I'm guessing.

'March the first. What's his favourite colour? Or band?'

I see her point so tell her she needs to be getting back to school.

My mum calls because she's forgotten I'm forty-two and feels compelled to check up on me whilst Bob is away. During her prolonged and one-sided call I continue to serve customers but I let the sausage rolls burn so I tell her I need to go.

'It's good to know that you've got Mark,' she says.

'What is this? Love Mark Week?'

'He'll help you cash up tonight. He's good with numbers.'

'And I'm not?'

'Well, no, love, you're not. You're good with customers. Everyone likes chatting to you, but we both know that you re-sat your maths GCSE twice.'

And still didn't get it. She doesn't add that. She's not a cruel woman.

It takes me an hour and a half to cash up at the end of the day. It normally takes Bob thirty minutes, but it balances and I'm encouraged to see the takings are healthy.

As I set the shop alarm, Mark turns up.

'All cashed up?'

'Yup.'

'Well done, love. I knew you'd do brilliantly. Here.'

He pushes a bunch of flowers under my nose: roses and the whimsically named baby's breath.

'They're gorgeous.' I give him a smacker even though I usually avoid public displays of affection. 'Pink's my favourite colour.'

'I know.'

'What's your favourite colour, Mark?'

'Blue.'

'And band?'

'Red Hot Chili Peppers.'

On the way home he lists his five favourite movies. We've three in common. Not bad.

Tuesday 24 October

When I said I'd look after the shop, I'd forgotten half term. I've had to farm out the kids to anyone who'll have them, or drag them into the shop. Oli's pleased and is living off custard slices but Libby's suddenly become a vegetarian and having her in the shop has been quite disruptive. Once she discovered that pretty much everything we sell contains animal fat, she set about telling the customers exactly how animal fat is processed from abattoir to bakery; it wasn't pretty to listen to. After losing three sales, I resort to giving her a fiver and sending her to the paper shop. As she leaves, I tell her what wine gums contain; she can damage their sales instead. Bob needs a business to come back to.

They're back tomorrow. They've been cruising up to Norway to see fjords and ice and things. Don't see the point myself. Might as well save cash and wait for winter; we're usually besieged by snow until about May round here. Besides, I'm not a water baby; feeding ducks in the park often makes me feel seasick. Actually, pretty much everything makes me feel sick at the moment. The choice of vitamins for menopause symptoms is confusing. There are tablets for itchy skin and thinning hair, others for headaches and tiredness, but none for nausea. I buy none and decide to visit the doctor.

I'm just completing the orders and debating whether I should cut back on apple pies but up the ante with vanilla slices when

Imogen calls. Imogen only ever calls if someone has died or I've done something she disapproves of. I answer with some wariness.

'Vicky has told me. How could you?' she hisses.

I search my mind for the root of her disapproval. Since I last saw Imogen I've visited a hairdresser and had blond stripes put in and I've bought a new winter coat. These two events are unusual but I cannot imagine either inciting her wrath.

'Gill from my DIY course recommended the hairdresser. Mum can't keep getting the scissors out – her hand isn't as steady as it was – and you're always saying I should take care of myself.'

'I'm not on about your haircut. That's good. I mean getting *pregnant*.'

'Pregnant?' I spurt the word out in surprise and hysteria. Oli stares at me suspiciously.

'Who's pregnant?' he demands.

'No one.' I take the phone into the back and whisper, 'What gave you such a mad idea?'

'Vicky said you called her and told her you have all the symptoms.'

'It's the menopause, early,' I hiss.

'Oh.' I hear the relief in her voice. No sympathy at my bidding farewell to my youth, I note. 'Thank God for that.' She hangs up.

I'm bouncing with gossipy-jump-to-conclusion Vicky. Will call her tonight and tell her to become a novelist: good use of vivid imagination.

We always shut up shop early on a Tuesday; Libby explains to Oli that this is a pre-war tradition: 'You know, like when Mum was a girl.' I'm too shattered to be offended, or to point out that was traditionally Wednesdays. We shut up shop early on a Tuesday because Bob visits his old mum and she's in a home where bingo is played on Tuesday afternoons. Anyway, I just want to go home, drink tea and eat biscuits but I feel the kids deserve some attention. Suddenly, once again, Mark appears like a genie – seemingly from nowhere – and offers to look after them for the afternoon to give me a break. I ask him who is converting the lofts of Leicestershire whilst he's skiving; he assures me that Terry can manage on his own. I seriously doubt this. Terry looks about the same age as Libby, though apparently he's twenty. But then nowadays policemen and footballers don't look old enough to tie their own boots.

I appreciate the offer but what would I do with myself if they all were out the house? We decide to visit the cinema together. Libby agrees as long as we all walk behind her by four paces. Oli, on the other hand, is really chuffed, particularly when we buy a family ticket. I like buying a family ticket too, but mostly because it saves three quid and they supersize the popcorn.

The moment the lights go down I fall asleep and I miss the entire film, only waking when the credits roll and Mark gently nudges me. I'm aware that there is saliva dribbling from my mouth, which is embarrassing. I don't think it's possible to be any more mortified but I'm proven wrong about that when Mark leans close to me and whispers, 'Maybe you should get a test done. Vicky might be right.' I stare at him too stunned to reply, besides which my mind is full of slow and painful ways I can torture and kill my ex best friend.

Tuesday 31 October

Halloween, and I'm fighting a few personal demons. Graham calls to ask when the kids' half term is.

'Last week,' I say crossly. I'd left him a series of messages asking if he could possibly help out on childcare; the kids would've liked to be at his place, where you can't spit without hitting a flat-screen TV. He never returned my calls.

'Oh, how disappointing, I'd have loved them to stay over for a couple of days.'

Clank, clank, what's that I hear? The rubbish men collecting the trash he shoots.

'Where were you last week?' I demand.

'The Canaries. It's the only place to get any sun this time of year.'

The kids would have *loved* that. I silently seethe. Suddenly, my week filled with mornings in the shop and afternoon trips to my mum's, the cinema and the swimming pool seems shoddy and inadequate. I wonder if I can protect the kids from ever hearing about Graham's holiday with the Usurper. Unlikely: they probably look Tangoed and will make everyone sit through a digital slide show of photos of the two of them drinking Bacardi.

'How's the course going?'

I'm enjoying it. I've met a few nice women and I like the feeling of independence that it's giving me. My only regret is that Graham instigated the idea and he's been unbearably smug ever since.

'It's OK,' I say sulkily, sounding a bit like Libby.

'I was wondering if you knew much about overflow. We've got a back-up.'

I can see that my saw skills could come in useful as I fantasise about cutting him up into little pieces and feeding him to wild boars (not that you get many wild boars round Leicestershire). Luckily the beep-beep of call waiting cuts our chat short. He's saved by the bell.

It's my mum. I moan that Graham can offer the kids more and leaves me feeling inadequate. She points out that whether he can offer them more or not, he never does so. I then confess to feeling jealous of Usurper's curtains. In fact I'm also jealous of her trim size-ten body, her clothes, the hours she spends in the beautician's and her foreign holidays, but I know I have the best chance of Mum relating if I stick to curtains.

'Stop looking over your shoulder at what Graham has, what

you might have had or what you once had and concentrate on the here and now. You'd be better for it. We all would.'

My mum rarely gets snappy with me, so I feel about an inch tall and get off the phone as quickly as possible.

She might have a point, so I nip out to the local veg shop and buy a pumpkin to carve for the kids. It'll be fun.

Two Elastoplasts and some very blue language later, I've carved a lopsided cat's face that looks comical rather than scary. I tell the children it was the effect I wanted so as not to scare toddlers. Both kids are enthusiastic about idea to go trick-or-treating; after all, free sweets are free sweets. They're less animated about the costumes I fashioned this afternoon. The party shop had been raided by the efficient mums who buy Halloween costumes in August, so my kids have to make do with old sheets and a bit of strategically placed black crêpe paper. Whilst we're out, Mark calls me on my mobile.

'Have you done the test yet?'

'There's no need.'

'Why, have you, er . . .'

'No, not yet. But I'm late because I'm menopausal and I wish everyone would stop going on about it. Why can't I sink into old age in dignified silence?' I ask with angry hisses. Luckily the kids are fighting over mini Mars bars and not paying me much attention.

'Robyn, you're too young to be menopausal. Besides, you look fabulous at the moment, positively glowing. You're being sick and you're late; those are signs of fertility, not the opposite. Why are you in denial? Would it be so awful?'

At that moment I see Libby rush across the road to catch up with her friends. She hardly glanced at the traffic.

'Libby, for goodness' sake, how many times do I have to tell you to be careful on roads?'

'Is that your answer?' asks Mark.

'No.'

'Well? Is the idea of being pregnant with my child so repugnant that you are in denial?'

It's a daft question. So I don't dignify it with an answer. About an eternity passes.

Mark coughs and then says, 'I see. Well, call me if you need anything.'

Then he hangs up.

Suddenly the ghosts and goblins look really scary.

Tuesday 7 November

Normally I love fireworks night, always have, even though it's always cold and drizzling. I love the smell of hot dogs and onions, the noise, the colour; it's exciting. But now and forever more I will associate it with blind terror.

I've done the test. Three times actually. If ever I've seen a woman on TV doing multiple tests I've thought it was blinking ridiculous. Those tests cost a fortune; no one in their right mind really wastes money double-checking the results. It says on the packet that it's 99.999999 per cent accurate or something. But I see now that's just it: people in their right mind. I'm not.

In my right mind, that is.

I *am* pregnant.

Despite my lack of maths GCSE, I'm able to calculate that I'm likely to be ten weeks' gone. When I was pregnant with Libby and Oli, my first reaction was to pick up the phone and tell everyone; this time my reaction is to hide in a darkened room, perhaps give birth secretly and pretend it is a foundling. What will the kids say? What will my family say? What will Mark say?!

Each question makes me feel sicker, which is an achievement of sorts, considering I feel round-the-clock pukey as it is. It takes two days before I even have the nerve to call Vicky.

'Congratulations. I knew it!'

'I didn't.'

'Really?'

'Really.'

'You were in denial?'

'Yes.'

'But you are pleased.'

'Well . . . yes and no. On a simple level, it's a new life – hurrah! More realistically, I'm an over-the-hill divorcee who thought the next pram I'd be pushing would be my grandchild's. I'm pretty sure my kids had the same view; their response will not be one of pure joy. Then there's my parents and sister, who are quaintly old-fashioned on such subjects. They'll feel duty-bound to draw attention to my unmarried status.'

'And Mark?'

'Mark has vanished.'

No sight nor sign for over a week. There's a big gap where he used to be. Oli's struggling with changing the tyre on his bike. Libby was miserable because we went to the local fireworks without him. She kept pointing out dads carrying kids on their shoulders even though, in heels, she's taller than I am and the scenario was never likely to occur, although I admit he'd have bought her a toffee apple. Then there's me.

I miss him. Unfair! After all my care and caution, it turns out that he has wormed his way under my skin. I set a place for him at tea last week, out of habit. I miss his chatter. I miss that he checks the doors are locked at night, even after I've done it. I miss his daft jokes and his impatience with politicians, which makes him shout at the TV. It's beginning to dawn on me that more than anything specific, I'm missing the opportunity that he was. 'And now there's a baby who will miss his dad more than anyone,' I say, fighting tears.

'Call him,' says Vicky.

I don't think I can. Having had a week to mull it over, I now see that I haven't been a great girlfriend. Despite Mark being a pretty good bloke and doing nothing to hurt me and quite a lot to make my life better, my wariness bordered on coldness and rudeness. I can't just call him now like some nineteenth-century fallen woman, desperate and alone.

The kids are at their dad's, so I crawl under the duvet and try to think what I should do next. I rub my stomach so that the poor little thing feels comforted. I don't want it to have any idea the trouble that will be coming with it.

The doorbell jolts me awake. Disorientated, I fight through the fog of deep slumber and stumble downstairs to answer it. It's probably Libby, forgotten an essential eyeliner or something.

It's Mark.

'Vicky called me.'

'Of course she did. Rent-a-gob.'

'Were you going to call me?'

'Eventually.'

'When? On its eighteenth birthday?'

'Before then. Come in, we can't discuss this on the doorstep.' I'm aware that in the next few months I'll give the neighbours plenty to gossip about. I'm keen to keep a low profile for as long as possible.

I got it wrong – again. I thought Graham was for life and infallible, but I was wrong about that, and then I thought Mark was a stopgap – the rebound – but maybe I'm wrong about that too.

He's male and therefore incapable of making long romantic speeches but when I told him that I thought he wouldn't want to know, he said, 'Daft cow,' but nicely. And when I told him I didn't know what to do next, he said we had plenty of time to think about names and I should put my feet up. He made me beans on toast with Cheddar melted on top and a splash of Worcester sauce. My favourite.

Tuesday 14 November

Mark's delighted and supportive response to the news of the baby gave me a momentary glimmering hope that being a forty-two-year-old single mum was going to be OK after all. Wrong again. True, at least I now know that I have his help, but I'm not out of the woods yet.

We decide that I need to see a midwife before we break the news to anyone. We make an appointment and the humiliation begins.

Co-parenting might be very modern and acceptable down south or in big cities, but here in a tiny village in Leicestershire, the midwife (Jane Davis, who I went to school with and have known forever) could not resist raising an eyebrow when she noted our separate names and addresses.

'And will these addresses be the same at the time of the birth?' She was as good as holding a shotgun to Mark's head. 'How's Graham, Robyn? I haven't seen him for a while.'

'You're a midwife,' I point out huffily. 'He's unlikely to be calling on your services.' It is not the moment to defend myself and tell Jane about the Usurper; after all, I'm flat on my back with my legs in stirrups and I've just handed over a pot of wee. It's hardly a position of strength.

'Well, having this baby won't be the same as the others,' she says glumly. 'You're a geriatric mum now.' I think she's joking until she goes on to tell me about lots of scary additional tests that are required because of my age. I feel woozy so Mark suggests we go for a drink. Jane scowls; he blushes and says he meant orange juice.

The conversation with my mum doesn't go much better.

'I'm pregnant.'

'Funny thing, dear, I thought you said you were pregnant,' she giggles. 'I must have my hearing checked.'

'I *am* pregnant.'

'When's the wedding?'

'We haven't talked about a wedding.'

'Give me Mark's address. I'll send your father round.'

Considering my dad was only five foot nine in his prime and weighs less than I did on my wedding day, and Mark is six foot one and beefy, I don't think this is a good idea – although it shows a certain sweetness in my parents' relationship. I tell Mum that I don't want to get married and that the baby, whilst unplanned, is still a cause for celebration, and that Mark and I will be very happy co-parenting from separate homes; after all, Graham and I do it with the other two. Mum tuts. She wants to be furious at me but is secretly excited at the idea of knitting booties and also hysterical because I used the term 'co-parenting' without sniggering (me, who has problems with the expression 'partner'), so she simply comments that she wonders what Imogen will have to say and then hangs up.

I don't have to break the news to Imogen, because Mum has Imogen on speed-dial, and by the time I call, I find Mum has already passed on the good news.

'You lied to me!'

'No, I was mistaken.'

'How could you be so stupid?'

It's a fair question, but because I'm hormonal I still take offence. 'It happens, Imogen!'

'Yes, to teenagers. Not to *old* women.'

I slam the phone down. If I'd been able, I'd have rammed it down her throat.

Mark and I buy in a KFC bucket and max-size everything so there is enough to feed an army. We encourage the children to drink pop and have seconds of ice cream; they are immediately suspicious.

'Are you splitting up?' asks Oli.

'No, no,' I reassure him, somewhat depressed by his line of reasoning.

'Are you pregnant?' Libby asks the question but then flings her head back and squeals with laughter. She clearly does not see it as a serious possibility.

'Er. Yes.'

The laughter stops.

'I hate you,' the children say in unison. To think that in the past I've prayed they'd agree on something.

'I thought you liked Mark,' I comment, somewhat clumsily considering he's in the room.

'We do. It's just that now everyone will know you've had sex,' says Libby, fighting tears.

'People might have assumed as much anyway. I'm only forty-two, Libby.' I try to stay reasonable.

'There's no *only* about it. You're ancient.'

'And disgusting,' adds Oli. 'I'm going to live at Dad's.'

I want to tell him that his dad has sex too, but I can't be that cruel.

They get up and march out of the room. Libby slams the door with extraordinary force; I watch a crack scamper from the frame across the ceiling.

'That didn't go too badly,' says Mark.

I ask him to pass the chips. I wish I was the sort of woman who ate less under stress.

Tuesday 21 November

Despite it being over a month until Christmas, the shops are stacked full of unnecessary bubble bath and chocolate boxes, indicating that this is the season to be jolly. I can't agree. Normally it's a magical time. I like everything about Christmas, from choosing, buying and wrapping pressies to cooking, overeating and overdrinking. I love my old Christmas tree, which I drag out of the loft every year, almost as much as I love my kids, and my Christmas dinners are unparalleled; even Imogen admits as much.

But this year I'm looking forward to Christmas about as much as the turkeys are. The atmosphere in our home is not what you'd call festive. At least Libby and Oli did not move out. They tried it, but after an evening of hearing the Usurper repeat, 'Well, who would have believed it?' they got bored and came home. There's no point in having flat-screen TV if you can't hear it above her hysteria. They're still not speaking to me, though; at least not beyond barking the odd instruction about what they want in their lunch boxes or asking whether such-and-such top is clean. In many ways it's situation normal, except I know they are hurt and confused and I've turned their world upside-down.

I try to talk to Libby about making the best of unexpected events. I confess to being secretly excited about the thought of once again attending tear-jerking nativity plays. Libby gawps at me with something akin to murderous fury.

'How would you like it if I came home pregnant?' she yells angrily.

'Not at all,' I admit. 'But you're thirteen.'

'And you are forty-two!' I really hadn't been aware of how ageist my family is. 'And you're not even getting married!'

Or how traditionalist.

The thing is, he hasn't asked me. I can't admit as much and risk her turning her loathing on to Mark, so I remain mute.

Mark has said that he wants to come to the antenatal classes, but we haven't discussed anything beyond that. I shouldn't care and I tell myself I don't. BUT I DO! I blame Christmas. It comes with unrealistic expectations. I'm plagued with thoughts of families sitting around hearths, even though everyone knows the best we can hope for nowadays is families squabbling around the remote control.

This year Christmas shopping is a chore. I'm so tired I look like the walking dead and I feel about as healthy too. I haven't had much actual sickness, just a constant feeling of nausea.

Imogen claims to have the same – she says it's the shame. She's resigned her position as PTA class rep because she says she won't be able to hold her head up in public when my news breaks. I sarcastically thank her for her support and ask if she kept any of Katie's baby equipment. I can't afford to hold a grudge. She says she'll check in the garage but isn't hopeful. She would like to cut me off completely but can't. It's my year to host Christmas; she hates cooking and would sup with the devil himself if it saved her from washing up.

Mum has muttered ominously that she's looking forward to Christmas dinner, as she'll be glad to have the opportunity to talk some sense into Mark. I can see it now: they'll turn up with a few pounds of potatoes and some carrots from Dad's allotment and offer them up as a dowry.

Money is tight now that I have the new baby to consider, and buying gifts on a budget for my disapproving family is not much fun at all. I trail around stores selling scarves and novelty cufflinks. I don't know anyone who wears either; still, it hasn't stopped me buying them in the past. Whilst I'm browsing, my brother John calls to ask me what he should buy Vicky for Christmas. Despite my normally hearing white noise when he says the name of his latest girl, I can't help but stumble over this one.

'As in my best friend, radio-foghorn Vicky?'

'One and the same.'

'In that case, buy her a gag.'

'Very funny. By the way, I'm bringing her to the annual chimp party on Christmas Day.'

I can't remember him ever bringing a date to Christmas dinner; he says it interferes with his digestion, by which I assume he means he can't allow the full and antisocial effects of sprouts to run their course. He must feel truly comfortable with Vicky. I'm mildly concerned that their continuing intimacy will lead to him finding out that when I was fifteen, I shinned down the drainpipe to meet Michael Walker for a date, but I guess I have bigger worries right now. I tell him that's fine and hang up.

I'm debating between a fake-fur hot-water-bottle cover and a Christmas cracker full of whisky miniatures for my father-out-law when I bump into Mark.

'What are you doing here?' I demand.

'Shopping.'

Of course he probably is, we are in a shop, but he looks shifty and I doubt him. I find myself furtively looking round to see if I can spot the leggy blonde he's secretly meeting.

'Who are you looking for?'

I'm too tired to fake it. 'Your mistress.'

Mark laughs. 'I love your sense of humour.' Then he clocks my stony expression. 'You're not joking, are you?'

'I've trained myself to expect the worst. I'm rarely disappointed.'

Irritation flashes across his face, but he subdues it and asks what I've bought. He's not impressed by my mittens for Mum or the luminous Santa for Imogen. I don't like that much either, and she'll hate it; that's its attraction. My mobile rings again: this time its Graham to say he and the Usurper are delighted to accept Libby's invite to Christmas dinner, plus he's bringing his parents. Obviously they all want to be in on the family crisis and gossip. It will be like Libby's birthday but worse, because now I'm a fallen woman and we'll all have to sit together and listen to the Queen's speech on traditional values. I can't even drink. I make a quick calculation and work out I'll be about sixteen weeks pregnant by then. The looking-fat-but-not-looking-pregnant stage – marvellous. I could kill Libby: this is clearly an act of war.

I hang up and start to quietly blub. Mark pulls me to his chest, which makes me feel better, which makes me feel worse. Hasn't he noticed that it's nice when we are together?

'Do you want to see what I bought?' He pulls out a voucher

for a day of pampering and personal shopper, plus credit, in the posh department store in town. 'It's for Libby, for Christmas.'

I'm bowled over by his thoughtfulness and his preparation: fancy, a man who Christmas-shops in November. Graham never bought Christmas presents, although I did get new carpets in the January sales every three years (he got a substantial staff discount). I bought for everyone else. Dad and John panic-buy from the petrol station on Christmas Eve. Mum has ten aerosol cans of de-icer, three torches and countless packets of those hanging air-freshener things. She's never ungrateful, though. She says she's the girl to know if ever you find yourself in a dark, snowy, smelly place.

'This is for Oli.'

'A belt?'

'A lead. And I thought we'd get him the dog to go with it. I know we have a lot on with the baby and things, but he really wants a dog. I'll walk it. Every family needs a dog.'

Oli has been pleading for months, but that last sentence from Mark swung it.

When we return from the pound with a bouncing pup (Labrador/bulldog cross, lord help us), Oli and Libby are at home watching TV. The scene would have been perfect if we'd interrupted them from studying, but hey, you have to be realistic.

Boy and dog jump excitedly around the kitchen, one shouting out a host of thank yous and the other dripping saliva on my lino. Even Libby manages a smile.

'What should we call her?' asks Oli.

'It's your dog, you choose,' I say.

'No, Mark can choose and I'll name the baby,' Oli says with a cheeky grin. This is the first thing he's said that so much as hints at him accepting or anticipating the baby, and he is clearly acknowledging Mark's part in persuading me to get the dog. He'll be grateful for ever.

'Nothing obvious like Snowy,' says Libby.

'The dog's not white, therefore Snowy isn't what you'd call obvious,' argues Oli.

'Except it's snowing,' says my daughter. We all rush to the window and silently huddle together. She's right. Suddenly Christmas seems closer and there's a sense of charm and enchantment in the air.

'What about Tiger?' suggests Oli.

'Too masculine,' says Libby. 'How about Daisy? Daisy Dog is nice.'

'Marie Mc,' says Mark, coughing.

I move away from the window and pour four mugs of tea. I pass them round and start to hunt in cupboards for the chocolate digestives. I hid them from myself in an attempt to curb the munchies.

'Oh yes, I prefer Marie to Daisy. How about we call the dog Daisy, and if the baby is a girl we'll call her Marie? If it's a boy, Oli gets to choose. That's fair, isn't it?'

The room is silent. Clearly everyone is wowed by my decisive and diplomatic solution.

'Marry me,' repeats Mark, clearer this time. He also reaches into the cupboard where we keep the DVDs and pulls out the chocolate digestives, which he offers me.

'Oh, oh I see.' I feel a bit thick. A bit thick and totally chuffed. I reach for a biscuit. 'Go on then.' I mean, why wouldn't I? 'I think maybe the dog should be called Lucky.' Because I am.

Tea And Sympathy

'So why here?' I ask as I plonk myself down, reach for a rusk and hand it to Charlie in the vain hope that it will keep him quiet at least long enough for Megan to answer the question.

I briefly worry about the sugar content of the snack as I sip on the cappuccino that Megan has already thoughtfully ordered. But the concern is mild compared to whether I'm stimulating my child enough to unleash all his potential, whether he'll ever make it to the top of the waiting list for my preferred school and whether I should have him inoculated in one fell swoop or mess around with three separate injections. Today's concerns. All of which are forgotten in light of Megan's – my best friend for ever – extraordinary behaviour.

This morning, she called me and insisted on a change of venue. It should be no big deal; we're only talking coffee shops. We meet weekly; our criteria aren't demanding. We simply need somewhere that won't actively loathe us for having children, that serves warmish beverages and that allows us to talk about the joyful insanity that is child-rearing. The extraordinary thing is that Megan called at 8.30 this morning and demanded that I get to her appointed café as soon as possible. 'It opens at nine,' she insisted. I told her I'd do my best to be there near ten. I used to be punctual; now I'm haphazard. I had planned on doing some cooking before I met up with Megan: organic chicken and vegetable stew for Charlie. I was going to freeze several tiny portions because having something wholesome in the freezer reduces potential stress at teatime. But Megan, normally reserved and accommodating, wouldn't hear of it. She actually *commanded* that I get to this particular café ASAP.

I look around. The café is on Highgate High Street; it's quaint but not prepossessing. I wonder if they serve good cakes.

'So why here?' I repeat.

As she tells me (no eye contact, fiddling with a tissue, beads of sweat on her upper lip), I think that it is too beautiful a day to receive news like this. The sun is shining and I'm dressed in just a T-shirt, no coat, although it's only April. This time last year we were damp-proofing the house and still wearing thermals.

'You must be mistaken. Caleb is away on business,' I say weakly.

It turns out that my best friend saw my husband in a restaurant last night, one local to here. He was holding another woman's hand. He helped her into her coat as they left the restaurant together.

'It was him,' replies Megan, quietly but firmly.

Megan looks terrible. There are dark shadows under her eyes and I notice for the first time that she has very deep crow's feet. She is thirty-four, the same age as me. She looks older. Her ten-month-old daughter has never slept a night through since she was born. Megan has always envied the fact that Charlie is a good sleeper. I sigh and wonder whether the baby was responsible for her sleepless night last night, or was it my husband's infidelity? Megan also envies the fact that I am now thinner than I was before I got pregnant, and that the house Caleb and I bought seven years ago has just sold for a massive profit. She never got on the property ladder and so she and her husband Robert throw huge sums of money at a landlord every month.

I feel sick.

Megan moves her coffee cup and nudges aside the half-eaten muffins and the soggy paper napkins that she's used to mop the various spillages that are part and parcel of the coffee-with-children experience. The debris suggests she has been waiting for me for some time. She discreetly lays her hand on top of mine, and squeezes tightly. Her hand is clammy. She's plainly extremely nervous. I bet she wishes that she and Robert hadn't chosen that particular little Italian last night. I could almost feel sorry for her, except I feel too sorry for myself to spare the emotion on anyone else.

'I've . . . we've,' she corrects, 'suspected for a while.'

I assume she is referring to her and dull Robert (Megan married the dull one, I married the fun one). But by 'we' she might mean any number of my friends; it might be all of north London. I don't know and I don't want to know.

'There's been talk, rumours.'

I want to tell her that there are always rumours. Our hands are constantly full with loads of dirty washing, babies and saucepans, but our minds are empty except for gossip and speculation. Except I know that I'm not being fair.

'I followed him. They went into that house over there.'

Megan points across the road to a terraced cottage, the type that is extremely prestigious to own and expensive to rent. It is clear that Caleb's mistress is wealthy. *And* her windows are clean. Both facts annoy me intensely. I stare at the door that Megan is pointing at. It's a cold blue colour. The brass knocker is huge, vulgar. The pretty window boxes – full of fashionable black tulips – enrage me.

'I thought perhaps she was his sister, but . . .'

She knows Caleb doesn't have a sister, so the conversation trails away. After a moment she finds inspiration enough to add, 'Or maybe just a good friend.'

I could declare that to be the case. Megan would believe me, or at least pretend to. And that would be enough. If she could pretend this conversation hadn't taken place, then I could too.

Easily.

Because I am good at pretending. I pretend to believe Caleb when he rings me to say he has to work late again or, like last night, that he has an overnight conference that he must attend. I pretend I believe him when I ask who he was talking to on the phone and he says it was a wrong number. I pretended to believe him when he told me that it was no longer company policy to take wives to the Christmas party. I've pretended so well that I had myself convinced.

It's as if Megan knows this, because she adds, 'He's still in there. His car is parked around the corner. I thought you'd need to see for yourself.'

I can't speak. If I open my mouth, I'll howl. I look at her, and with difficulty she meets my gaze.

'It's probably just sex. If they have, you know, had sex . . . that's all there will be to it.' She sighs, recognising the inadequacy of her flimsy excuses for my husband. 'Did I do the right thing by telling you?' she asks.

She's really asking do I hate her or him? Megan has baby spew on her cardigan. Her daughter is a sicky baby; she can't keep anything down. Charlie's very neat. It is good luck, not good management, if you end up with a baby that doesn't puke up everything you force down it. Megan has never believed that. She thinks I have a magic formula that helps me be a more pristine mum and envies me for that.

I nod, as I still can't trust myself to speak.

'So what are you going to do now?' Her face is contorted with the peculiar cocktail of relief and concern; it's devoid of envy.

I gather up the baby paraphernalia. Charlie's comfort blanket, which is as filthy as it is loved, his beaker, the nappy bag, his

76

dummy. I carefully put these essentials away and then gently cajole Charlie into his buggy.

As I pass out through the café door, it is as though I have two choices. I could go home and make the casserole, or . . .

I lift the vulgar knocker and rap it hard against the blue paintwork of Caleb's mistress's door. The pretending has to stop: his and mine. I'm going to make more than stew this morning.

Easy One-Pot Chicken

Makes 12 portions (for a baby!)
½ small onion, finely chopped
15 g/½ oz butter
100 g/4 oz chicken breast, cut into chunks
1 medium carrot, trimmed and sliced
275 g/10 oz sweet potato, peeled and chopped
300 ml/10 oz chicken stock

Sauté the onion in butter until softened. Add the chicken breast and sauté for 3–4 minutes. Add the vegetables, pour over the stock, bring to the boil and simmer, covered, for about 30 minutes or until the chicken is cooked through and the vegetables are tender. Purée in a blender to the desired consistency.

A Rose By Any Other Name
Would Smell As Sweet

'I'm thinking of throwing a Valentine's party this year,' said Sophie, dishing up a big, innocent grin.

'You're kidding, right?'

'More partying is in everyone's interest.'

Jane sighed and looked at her sister with a blatant mix of accusation and incredulity. 'You've hosted three birthday parties this year. Why would you even think of having another party?'

'They were for the kids. I want to throw a party for grown ups. I mean adults.' Sophie corrected herself. The adults she knew were not all grown up; that was her point.

Jane felt sick. This was the most ridiculous and painful idea her well-intentioned, but woefully misguided, sister had come up with yet. Valentine's Day! Jane's own private hell. There were the two words most likely to strike fear into her heart; crueller than 'facial hair', more uncomfortable-making than 'smear examination'. Jane did not have children to throw birthday parties for. Nor did she have a husband or even a boyfriend. She had been engaged once, in her early twenties. They'd split up before the wedding. On Valentine's Day. To coin an old-fashioned phrase, she'd jilted him. Sometimes, when she looked back on her actions, she struggled to remember them with absolute clarity, she laboured to justify them. She remembered feeling panicked that the wedding planning was cutting into far too much of her studying time; she had her exams to think of, and she remembered thinking that Mark was a nice enough guy, but that nice enough wasn't enough. Although it wasn't clear what *exactly* might be enough for Jane. It was all such a long time ago. She'd since dated various men, on and off, but she'd never committed. Sexy, bad boy types disappointed her, she ridiculed and distrusted devoted romantics and she dismissed any one in between as 'Boring, far too normal.'

'What are you looking for?' Sophie often asked, exasperated.

'Just someone who understands I have a career and friends of my own. Someone who has that too, but wants to share.' Jane didn't think this was too much to ask. It seemed practical and sensible, so it should be possible. Jane was all about the practical and sensible; admittedly she gave less thought to what was possible.

Her mother had never quite forgiven her. 'What sort of girl calls off her wedding on Valentine's Day?' she'd yelled. 'You've ruined your one chance of happiness.'

Jane thought her mother was wrong about her ruining her one chance of happiness. It simply wasn't true. Jane was happy. At least, she felt very content, which was a lot like happiness. She had a full life. She was a solicitor and would probably make partner next year; all her studying and hard work had paid off. She went to gigs with the frequency of a teenager, she had good friends, two dogs – not cats, she'd resisted becoming a cliché – and a stylish home. A home in which she was free to eat whatever she liked, whenever she liked and to watch anything she pleased on TV. Microwave meals for one and uninterrupted viewing of *The Walking Dead* were sufficiently compensatory. The only time that she found being single difficult, and contentment elusive, was on Valentine's Day.

On February 14th, Jane felt like her life was an enormous black hole; no matter how many computer literacy or yoga classes she fitted in, committees she sat on or hours she spent in the office, she could not fill that day. She found herself dwelling on the fact that every other woman in the United Kingdom was wearing silky underwear, under a new, fabulous dress, eating a delicious meal by candlelight and drinking vintage champagne whilst her husband or boyfriend serenaded her and threw red rose petals in her path. Jane told herself that Valentine's Day was actually, simply a materialistic, manufactured, almost grotesque commercial enterprise, but the image of a more beautiful and romantic version of the day, largely manufactured by glossy, glorious magazines, always chewed its way into her consciousness and, furtively, she longed for it.

Not that she'd ever admit such a thing. If there was one thing a single girl understood the importance of it was saving face.

'Well, count me out,' declared Jane.

'Have plans, do you?' asked Sophie.

Jane glared at her. 'No one will come anyway. Don't couples want time to themselves on Valentine's Day? Isn't that the point?'

'I don't *just* know couples.' Actually, Sophie's friends were mostly couples but she thought they would rally when they heard her plan; all her friends were aware of Jane's singledom.

'Why would you want a bunch of drunks staggering around your house and throwing up in the cloakroom?'

Sophie laughed at Jane, refusing to be put off. 'It won't be like that. I'm going to have a romantic theme and ask everyone to wear pink.'

'Even the men?'

'I'll serve salmon canapés and rose cava.'

'You'll find it spilt on your new cream sofa.'

Sophie ignored her. 'I'll have a chocolate fountain.'

'Chocolate is not pink, it's not theme appropriate,' pointed out Jane churlishly.

'Don't be such a spoilsport, Aunt Jane. A party is a marvellous idea. You might meet someone and find luuurvvve!' Isobel, Sophie's eldest, interrupted the conversation. She had a habit of sneaking up on her aunt and mother when they were chatting. She'd found eavesdropping a tremendous source of information since she was an infant.

'No, I won't,' said Jane. 'I believe in "luuurvvve" less than I believe in Santa Claus or the Easter Bunny.'

'Don't let George hear you. He wavered in his belief this year.'

'At least George is eight. Your mother told me Santa didn't exist when I was three!' The outrage in Jane's voice was as crystal clear now as it had been back when the truth was first revealed.

Sophie cringed inwardly. She'd only been seven when she blurted out her discovery that the man who filled the stockings was their dad and that the elves that produced the gifts didn't exist, it was their mum who spent weeks from November trailing the stores for treats. Sophie had spent her life trying to make up for the faux pas that robbed her sister of her innocence. Sometimes, Sophie worried that the early disillusionment was the reason behind Jane growing up to be such a pragmatist. She was so sensible, rational and logical which was, in Sophie's opinion, the real reason she'd never fallen in love. To do so, you had to give a little. In fact you had to give a lot. You had to trust, hope and lose control.

Sophie didn't think that being married was the only way to find happiness, but it was the way *she'd* found happiness. She, Robert and their three children already had '*it*'. They were healthy, loved and loving. Between them they formed that enigmatic and enviable thing – a happy family. Of course they squabbled, snapped and sniped at one another from time to time. There had been that very worrying period when Isobel became secretive and dated unsuitable boys. George was dyslexic, which had its challenges and Sarah, the middle child, had started to cuss this year, repeatedly and ferociously, just to see if she got a reaction.

But most of the time they were one another's heart's ease. Magic dust. Happiness. Call 'it' what you will.

Sophie wanted more of the same for her sister. Jane had the bigger home in the smarter part of town, a career, foreign holidays, a wardrobe to die for and Sophie had a demanding family whose needs had long since drowned out her own desires. Unfashionably, she had no problem with that. She believed it to be the natural order of things. Her own mother had always made Sophie and Jane a priority.

Sophie had suggested that her sister try blind dating.

'I don't know anyone who knows anyone who's single any more! Who could fix me up?'

'Well, then, internet dating.'

'I'm not in the market to meet psychos.'

'Speed dating?'

'I have to enter into enough high-pressure pitches at work, thank you. I don't want that sort of nonsense intruding on my private life.'

So Sophie had decided to go back to basics. The good old-fashioned method of meeting people at parties.

Sophie made a huge effort with the party. She blew a silly amount of cash on rose cava and she baked and cleaned for hours. She nearly passed out blowing up pink balloons and she decked the kitchen, living room and hall with enormous red crêpe paper hearts. She was very strict about the entrance policy. Not only did she insist that her guests wear red or pink, she also explained that, instead of having to bring a bottle, every couple had to bring a spare man.

Her friends were surprised but, after a little cajoling, they agreed to the stipulation. After all, it was Valentine's Day; generally, most women are secret matchmakers and delighted in the possibility of being responsible for new love blossoming even if it did mean they had to sacrifice a romantic meal in the local restaurant.

Finally, the big day arrived. Sophie could not have been more excited. It was, as she'd expected, lovely to see her friends discard their coats, hats, scarves and gloves and melt in the warmth that her home oozed, but it was especially exciting to see the number of single men that had been brought along. She quickly assessed them, as though it was a beauty contest. At least two were especially handsome men, four had friendly smiles, the rest were passable – they probably had lovely personalities. Only one chap stuck out like a sore thumb. He was sitting on his own, not drinking the frothy cava but instead sticking with tap water; he wasn't wearing so much as a red tie or pair of socks, he was dressed in jeans and a grey jumper; he was not even faking an interest in the conversations around him, the only person he deigned to speak with was Isobel.

Jane was late.

'The invite said seven thirty,' scolded Sophie as she took her sister's coat. She noticed that Jane had ignored the dress code too. She was wearing black as though she was at a funeral. Sophie shoved her towards the kitchen, where the party (like all parties) was thriving. 'Tadarrrr.'

'What?'

'What's different about this party?' prompted Sophie.

Jane looked around the kitchen. It was heaving. There were a lot of men, which was a bit odd; normally at parties the women stayed in the kitchen and the men hung around the iPad.

She hazarded a guess, 'Decent food?'

'Men!'

'What?'

'These are all single men. I asked my guests to bring a single man rather than a bottle. I asked them all to play Cupid to you.'

Sophie beamed. 'Most of them know about your broken engagement and everything, so they were really sympathetic.'

Jane stared at her sister in horror. How could she be so cruel? So thoughtless. The humiliation was intense; a hot blush was already forming on Jane's neck. Valentine's had always been ghastly when Jane was privately fighting her demons about the lack of a picture-perfect scenario – flowers and hearts, hubby and kiddies – but it had been bearable. Now Sophie had outed her, the mortification was overwhelming. Jane turned, grabbed her coat and ran. She didn't notice that she'd dropped her glove. She had to get out of the stifling house full of pitying and patronising couples.

Jane nearly slipped on the icy path. She stopped at the gate, fighting angry tears; she had never felt so alone.

'Excuse me.'

Oh God, that was the last thing she needed. Someone had followed her out of the house. Jane pretended she couldn't hear him calling to her and she began to walk along the street.

The man jogged to catch up. 'You dropped a glove,' he called. Normally, Jane loved her soft, beige buckskin gloves; right now, she hated them.

'Thank you.' She refused to meet his eye.

'I saw your dramatic exit. Very Cinderella.'

'I don't believe in fairy tales,' she said stiffly. 'Not even on Valentine's Day.'

'Nor do I. *Especially* not on Valentine's Day. I hate it. The sickest day of the year.'

Jane looked up, startled. It was refreshing, although somewhat surprising, to find someone else who was equally vitriolic about the day. She'd always found that there was a deep and dark silence surrounding the gloomy reality of the day. Single women simply dared not roll their eyes at the torturous nylon basques that seeped from every shop window, even though it seemed that the sole purpose of such garments was to humiliate flat-chested and saggy-bummed, aka normal, women.

'Do you know what I most hate about it?' he asked.

'The pink, plastic "I Love You" stamps for toast and similar plethora of tack which are no doubt mass-produced by children working in illegal conditions?' Jane wondered whether she sounded bitter and defeatist.

'Ha, no. Although that is offensive. It's my birthday too.'

'You're kidding?'

'Wish I was.'

Jane took the glove. 'So why do you hate it then? I'd have thought it being your birthday made it tolerable. At least you're guaranteed cards.'

He smiled wanly but didn't answer her question. 'I'll walk with you, if you're going to the tube station.'

Jane stole a glance. The guy didn't look like a psycho. 'Where are you going?'

'Err, embarrassing thing is, nowhere. So I've got time to squander. It's my birthday *and* Valentine's Day and yet I have some time to kill until my sister-in-law and brother emerge from the party. Then I'm staying with them for the weekend. I think they thought if they took me along to that party, then all their duties towards me, in terms of celebrating my birthday, were null and void. It's always such a disappointing day.' The man grinned as he made this awful admission. Jane noticed he had nice eyes. Particularly attractive when he grinned.

'Isn't it?'

'What were you hurrying from?'

'All of it.'

'I see.' They both fell silent. It was a comfortable silence. Jane realised she was enjoying the peaceful company of her fellow anti-romantic. He sighed deeply, his hot breath clouding the cold

night air. 'I know you think you are having a bad night but somewhere in that house, something truly awful is happening.'

'What?' Jane asked.

'I was talking to this teenager. Her mother has set up this
whole party to try to off-load some maiden aunt.'

Jane gasped. 'How terrible.'

'Isn't it? I told the girl her mother shouldn't be so interfering
and pushy. Just because it's Valentine's Day doesn't mean the
maiden aunt is suddenly going to find love or even want it. It's
such an imposition.'

Jane nodded. Mute with shock and embarrassment. She
couldn't let this cute guy know that she was the spinster aunt.
Because he was, well, a cute guy. He had full lips and lovely curly
hair. And a cynical side that she appreciated.

'What did the teenager say?' Jane knew that the forthright
Isobel would have expressed an opinion.

He grinned at the memory of the bolshie teenager, dressing
him down. 'She said I was a miserable devil. She said her mother
was only trying to help and that she *did* believe things were
different on Valentine's Day; that there is a little more magic
everywhere and, of course, the aunt wanted to find love.'

'Teenagers,' said Jane, tutting. 'So damned optimistic.'

They both fell silent again.

'Look, would you like to go for a drink? No bubbles though
– anything but that.'

Jane considered it. Maybe. She quite liked him. She liked his
sensible attitude to Valentine's Day. She was so fed up of people
insisting that it was a romantic, enchanted time. It's just another
date on the calendar. It was his birthday after all. No one wanted
to be alone on their birthdays.

'I'm Jane.' She held out her hand, he shook it.

'Pleased to meet you, Jane.' Jane waited for him to volunteer
his name. He didn't.

'And you are?'

'OK, well, this is it, I suppose. Crunch time. So it's my birthday today, right?'

'Yes, you said.'

'I'm Valentino Lovelass.' Jane snorted with laughter. 'What's funny?' he asked with mock incredulity.

'Nothing, nothing at all.' Jane was practically choking on her laughter. 'Are you joking?' she asked eventually.

'I never joke. I'm eminently sensible and practical. I'm always serious.' There was a glint in his eyes that belied the fact that he was always serious so Jane insisted he produce his driving license to prove he wasn't making up a ridiculous alias.

'I do at least understand why you hate Valentine's Day,' she said as they set off towards the pub.

'And my parents too – don't underestimate how much I hate them,' he joked.

'Oh get over it.' Jane laughed. Teasingly she added, 'It's not like they destroyed your belief in Santa Claus at an early age.'

'True, that would be really bad. Very bad indeed.'

Sophie and Isobel were watching from Isobel's bedroom window. Sophie winked at her daughter. 'Perfect,' she sighed.

'You are a regular Cupid, Mum. Congratulations. You do know his name though, right?'

'Oh yes. And how I'm going to enjoy hearing my sister introduce him!'

Adele Shares . . .

My Favourite Holiday Destinations

Oooh, this is a tricky one because there are loads of awesome places to travel to and have fun at. If pushed, I think I'd have to say (or perhaps yell) I love LA! It's so seriously glam and yet also chilled. My experience is that in LA everything is possible, positive and purposeful; I know this contradicts the stereotype image of the city and its people but I've found enormous warmth there. There's so much to do there and practically every footstep you take will place you on a movie set. If you want some beach time go to Santa Monica beach and pier, I love mooching around the fabulous flower market (although this does demand an early start!), Griffin Park is glorious, the stunning Getty museum is awesome, the theme parks are simply fun and if you want to catch a movie (and who doesn't in LA), then you have to go to the Chinese Theatre for old-school glamour. My family and I have returned over and over. It's impossible to become bored. Our secret tip for creative but unpretentious international comfort food is The Restaurant at The Standard, Hollywood. It's open twenty-four hours which is useful and we've only ever been delighted by the food and the service, which I'd describe as effervescent and efficient and, yes, of course, all the waiters want to be actors.

A bit closer to home is Rome. I first visited there when I was twenty-two and I was immediately and fatally seduced by this city of noise, chaos, energy and spirit. A city of contradictions and yet effortless conciliation; the ancient and modern bump up against one another, the old and the young get along, the frantic and the indolent coexist. Everyone is always in a hurry, except that is, when they're not. It's a city full of joy, laughter, rumour and chat. I like to watch the women in high heels and tight belts and who laugh in gaggles yet manage to attain a level of sophistication normally monopolised by catwalk models. I like to see nuns fluttering by or a priest puffing on a cigar, the achingly hip scoot and toot from their pastel coloured Vespas. I enjoy the passeggiata parade at five o'clock, when families dress up to simply walk together, kids chase pigeons, men throw appreciative glances at pretty women, the older Italians chatter and wink conspiratorially – they've seen it all before. It seems to me that the Romans know how to squeeze every ounce of juice out of life and after a visit there I always ask myself *perché non*. Why not, indeed!

Where are you off to? Let me know
@adeleparks #LoveIsAJourney

NEW BEGINNINGS

The Invitation

Ella's transfer from the Liverpool office to the smaller office in Chester had come along at exactly the right time, and she knew she had to maximise the opportunity. She'd promised herself that she'd accept every invite that fluttered her way. So far this meant she'd had to dig out flat shoes and amble around Westminster Park (commenting on the impressive landscaping), go to the Monday quiz night at the Crown (to answer questions on sport and politics) and get up early on a Sunday morning to play badminton (even though she hadn't held a racquet since she was in sixth form, nearly twenty years ago). She had not allowed for shyness or even personal taste.

In Liverpool, Ella had been stuck in a rut – emotionally and professionally – for far too long. The place was rammed with haunting memories of her ex, Peter, even though they'd divorced three years ago. She had occasionally dated since then, because everybody from her mother to her best friend to her teenage nieces said she ought to, but her broken heart wasn't in it and the men she went out with soon became aware of this. A clean start was exactly what was required. She needed to know that she could confidently walk around Waitrose without bumping into Peter and his new wife; she wanted to be able to go to a bar or restaurant without being bludgeoned with memories of times when she'd visited the same place as half of a happy couple.

The only problem was, despite the undoubted efficiency of the company's relocations department, a clean start required a lot of effort. The relocations manager had shown Ella four equally lovely one-bed apartments; she'd settled on the one nearest the park because she was thinking about getting a dog, or a bike, or something that would indicate that she had a life. The relocations manager registered her at a doctor's and a dentist's surgery; she even supplied a list of decent hair salons. The difficulty was acquiring new friends. Ella realised that she had to make some, but she secretly felt a little bit old for it. It was easy when you were eight: you simply shared your Curly Wurly or offered to turn the skipping rope. Not so easy at thirty-eight. The relocations manager couldn't help her with that one.

At work, a woman called Louise swept Ella under her wing. Ella gratefully snuggled there because they were the same grade middle management, the same age, and when they selected their lunches in the canteen, it transpired that they had the same taste in yogurts. Ella hoped it was enough to kick-start a friendship. The notable differences between them were that Louise was married with two sons, and she lived in a large town house. She was so proud of her husband, boys and house that she threw elaborate dinner parties every Saturday so that she could share her good fortune, and no doubt showcase it too, Ella thought, as she tried not to feel aggrieved by the glaring disparity.

Louise invited Ella for dinner. All week she chattered excitedly about the menu and the other guests. She was planning on serving monkfish and scallops with wood-roasted vegetables. She would also be serving up an eligible man for Ella's delectation. Ella knew the dinner party formula: three couples, her and a spare man. The marrieds looked to the singletons for entertainment. Would they or wouldn't they share a taxi home? Her married pals back in Liverpool had done exactly the same thing: potential boyfriends were recruited with Kitchener enthusiasm. Ella knew their intentions were good, and that a happily married woman like Louise was simply unable to resist matchmaking. It didn't stop her from dreading the evening.

It turned out to be exactly as expected. The food was marvellous, the guests were pleasant but not profound and the spare man was disinterested, possibly even gay. Conversation centred round children's schools and the difficulty in securing a trustworthy builder. They drank moderately because no one wanted a hangover; they couldn't afford to lose their Sunday mornings to such messiness. Those days had gone for these mums and dads. Ella went through the motions; these concerns weren't hers, but she was sympathetic and familiar enough with them to make the appropriate comments in the correct places. The only surprise was Louise's husband, Ned.

Ella had been expecting someone approaching middle age, a guy fighting his paunch and the weight of his mortgage. But in fact Louise's husband was quite exceptionally striking: classically tall, dark and handsome, with cheekbones you could cut yourself on. Ella would never, ever look at a man who was taken – she herself had been on the wrong end of infidelity; however, she couldn't fail to be impressed.

Until she talked to him. Ned was a bit dull for her tastes. He was perfectly pleasant, not rude or aggressive or overwhelmingly cocksure (frankly, any of those alternatives might have been more exciting); he was simply boring. He spoke for fifteen uninterrupted minutes about the best garden weedkiller available on the market. Louise beamed throughout his monologue, seemingly unaware that her guests had nodded off. When they said good night, she pulled Ella into a hug and whispered, 'I know that one day you'll find someone just as wonderfully dependable as my Ned.' Ella appreciated the sentiment and therefore bit her tongue, resisting commenting that she'd prefer to stay single than suffer a slow death by tedium, even if her killer was so utterly handsome. Each to their own, she thought, as she got in the back of the cab.

The next invite Ella received was from Evelyn in Accounts, who asked her to join a gang of colleagues for a drink in town. When Louise heard that it would be at Hooper's bar, she looked concerned.

'It's a cattle market. That place attracts the wrong sort.'

'Which sort, exactly?'

'People just out for a good time, if you know what I mean.'

Ella thought that people just out for a good time would be a welcome break from people who had forgotten how to have a good time, and so promptly accepted Evelyn's invite.

As she pushed open the door to the packed wine bar, she was hit by the smell of bodies and booze, by loud music and equally loud shirts. Everyone there was clearly jacked up on irresponsibility, a powerful aphrodisiac. Ella hadn't been to this kind of bar, full of intensely alluring types, for ages. It was in a place like this that she'd first met Peter, a lifetime ago. She was just thinking that she might very well enjoy herself for the novelty factor alone when she saw him, sitting at the bar surrounded by a bevy of young blondes, clearly having the time of his life. Ned.

She didn't stay long after that. Just long enough to see Ned slide his arm around the most attractive girl's waist. Her blood slowed. Poor Louise, poor trusting, content, loving Louise. After Peter had left Ella and the storm of tears and regrets had finally subsided, two of her friends came forward and said they'd long since suspected him of having an affair; one said she'd actually seen him with the other woman. Ella had felt betrayed all over again. Why hadn't they told her? Warned her? Prepared her? Her friends had muttered something about messengers being shot. She hadn't understood at the time, but now she did. She didn't want to be the one to bring the bad news to Louise's door.

The following week Ella reluctantly agreed to a blind date with her new dentist's brother. Her reluctance was fuelled by the fact that she doubted the success of this particular path to true love – it usually led to a dead end – but she acquiesced because every invite had to be honoured. As she scampered into the restaurant and out of the rain, she literally bumped into Ned. This time he was with a brunette, who was throwing her head back and screaming with laughter. Ella couldn't imagine what Ned might have said that was so funny.

'Sorry,' he murmured to Ella as she wobbled with the force of their collision. 'You OK?' He flashed the most charming smile and it didn't falter even when he stared right at her. In fact, in the moment when he must have registered who it was he'd bumped into, Ned's smile broadened a fraction further. The rat. Ella was struck dumb by his audacity and watched helplessly as he hailed a taxi and drove away with his brunette.

Naturally, the blind date was unsuccessful. Ella was in turmoil. Louise's husband was not having an affair; he was a serial philanderer! Poor Louise, those poor little boys. What could Ella do? After lengthy consideration, she decided that when she next spotted Ned, she'd tackle him. Make him see that his careless womanising was unacceptable. That it was in fact a declaration of war.

She didn't have to wait long. The following Thursday, she agreed to go for a drink with a group of women from her bums-and-tums class. They selected a quiet wine bar where it was possible to hold a conversation; mellow lounge music floated past the enormous potted plants and there was a menu of wines to savour. Ella thought it was a great find, until she spotted him.

This time he was with a stunning redhead. It was heinous to admit that they made a striking couple, yet brilliant to note that the date was clearly going badly. Ned kept looking at his watch and the redhead seemed more interested in the menu than him. Ella slunk behind a potted plant and bided her time. After just fifteen minutes, the redhead stood up, coolly kissed Ned on the cheek and said her goodbyes. Ella felt a jolt of delight and relief that tonight, at least, Ned hadn't got lucky. Would he now scuttle home to Louise? It wasn't a comforting thought, but what was the solution? As Ned waved for the bill, Ella grabbed her courage and the moment.

She stood in front of him, hands on hips. 'How could you?' she demanded.

'Sorry?' Ned had the nerve to look unperturbed.

'What do you think you are playing at? A small town such as this, you were bound to be spotted sooner rather than later. Not that you seem to be making much of an attempt at discretion.'

'I really think that—'

Ella cut him off. She'd heard all the excuses and clichés when she and Peter were splitting; she didn't want to hear them again. She wasn't going to allow another woman to suffer in the same way she had. So Ned was amazingly good-looking, and, considering how he'd been chatting to the blondes in Hooper's and the brunette at the restaurant, quite clearly gifted with some sort of charm (although she hadn't been enthralled at his dinner party); well, good looks and charm shouldn't automatically lead to infidelity. It was vile. He didn't even have the decency to look ashamed. He appeared unconcerned although mildly confused by Ella's outburst.

'It's the blatancy, the cruel indifference to Louise that I find most shocking.'

'Oh, you're a friend of Louise's.' Ned's face cleared.

'Ned, we met at your house. Am I that forgettable?' she demanded angrily.

'You're very memorable. And now I see you are also loyal,

feisty and beautiful.' Ella was incensed. Ned was hitting on her too now! How dare he? 'But I'm not Ned. I'm Ben, Ned's twin brother. Single brother,' he added with a delicious slow smile that thumped Ella in the stomach.

'Oh. I thought . . .' Ella faltered, embarrassed, delighted and excited all at once.

Ben's smile broadened a fraction further. 'Yes, I can imagine what you thought. Now, I wonder, would you like a drink?'

Ella accepted. After all, she had promised herself that she'd accept every invite that came her way. It would be wrong not to.

Flung

Whilst standing in an endless line for tickets at Victoria Station, it hits me that, likely as not, right now Donald and Amelia will be deciding between beach and pool. The most exciting decision I have in front of me is cheap day return versus an open ticket. I sigh and look down at my scruffy rucksack. Life's so unfair. I bet Amelia has a matching set of Louis Vuitton. Apart from the emotional baggage, I am travelling light. I'm wearing my bikini under my sundress and I've packed my toothbrush and a clean pair of knickers because I want to be wild and spontaneous (but clean).

Hi, bruv. How goes it? . . . Good, good . . . Me? Awful since you ask. He's dumped me . . . Yes, I know Donald Drake *is* a stupid name. I admit that . . . Very funny. Yes. I'm sure that you've been saving up the Disney jokes since I met him, haven't you? My line's bleeping. I'll call you later.

My mobile phone is warm in my hand and, if there is any truth to the theory that it emits brain-frying waves, then I suspect my brain is well and truly frazzled. It has been attached to my head more or less constantly for four days.

Hi, Jenni . . . Oh, I'm OK. You heard. Who told you? . . .
Liv. Well, saves me putting an announcement in the paper
. . . Devastated, obviously. I mean, single at thirty is bad
. . . What? Yes, admittedly he has a stupid name. But he
also has the cutest smile and up until ninety-six hours ago
was the custodian of my heart! . . . Oh, you were right . . .
Yup. Amelia in Accounts. She seduced him with her dinky
little embroidered slip dresses and *definitely* non-work-
place-appropriate strappy sandals . . .

The woman in the queue behind me gives me a sympathetic
smile-cum-grimace. I acknowledge her sympathy with a hound-dog
expression that I've perfected over the last few days.

Yes, I know it takes two to tango . . . I thought you said he
was perfect for me . . . Oh, and now 'you never liked him'.
Thanks . . . Yes, he is a bastard. It is bad . . . The added
humiliation is that the once-in-a-lifetime holiday to the
Caribbean that we'd planned together, saved for together
and booked together left with him! And can you believe he
offered to buy me out so that Amelia could go instead? . . .
Exactly, a bastard.

The queue moves forward. The guy in front of me is Italian. He
is communicating his desire for a one-way ticket on the Gatwick
Express by gesticulating madly. It puts me in mind of the histri-
onics I displayed as Donald tried to leave. I blush as I remember
clinging to his trouser legs, begging him to reconsider. It was
obvious that a relaxed, new-millennium, adult approach to parting
was not an available option. Sharing a bedroom platonically was
out of the question (although arguably we had managed this
successfully for the last six months of our relationship). I wanted
to tell him to sod off. To keep his money and his crappy holiday.

I wanted to mean it.

But as I am an underpaid assistant in a small PR agency, with barely a foot on the first rung of the corporate ladder, decadent displays of passion are not practical. I'm waiting for his cheque to clear.

I pull myself out of my self-pity and tune back in to Jen, who is still chatting merrily on the mobile.

You're right. He was an arrogant, self-absorbed git . . . He's never been that sensational in bed . . . I can't concede the point on flings, though. Oh Jen, they waste time . . . I'm sure that couples counselling does increase after the holiday period . . . Yes, it could be seen as an advantage that I have avoided that, but . . . What is my problem? I was kidding, I don't really want to hear . . . I don't see a string of long-term relationships that transition seamlessly into one another as a problem . . . Well, yes, Donald could be a wanker on occasion, but . . . Yes . . . Yes, I suppose I would have married him if he'd suggested it . . . It's not obscene. I know it's character-building, but I'm pretty happy with a lightweight character . . . Thirties are *not* great years . . . I haven't been freed from the insecurities that plagued my twenties . . .

Then, as now, I had an overwhelming fear of dying alone, losing my battle against orange-peel thighs and underachieving at work.

No, I haven't tried the Clarins one. Does it really work? I'll give it a go? Look, got to ring off; I'm near the front of the queue. Yeah, love you too. Thanks . . . Absolutely. Like a fish needs a bicycle.

I go for it, open return. It's the least I can do to honour my promise to my mum. After Donald did the dirty deed, I dished him to all my friends, ripped up his letters and photos and then climbed into the fridge to see if there was any comfort to be found. There wasn't. So I called my mum. I told her about my plans to spend a week alone, detoxing, sleeping, recuperating. She talked about more pebbles on beaches. I mumbled and sniffled, explaining that I'd spent hours perfecting my Pinterest board of Vera Wang and Jenny Packham dresses and all that time was wasted! She snapped and switched her wise words from 'fish in the sea' to 'cart before the horse'. She told me that it was a mistake to start choosing the children's names before the second round on a first date. It's serious when your mum encourages you towards casual sex.

I am on a lifelong search for Mr Right and historically I have not had time for flings. My CV is as follows: age fourteen to seventeen – exclusive to Dom. Age seventeen to nineteen – devoted to Ivan. Age nineteen to twenty-three – adored Paddy. Age twenty-three to twenty-six – attached to Giles. Age twenty-six to twenty-eight – passed time with Richard. Age twenty-eight to thirty and a half (and those six months are significant) – stayed with Donald. Over half my life wasted. Wasted, that is, if you consider my end goal: a small blue Tiffany box and a large white dress.

I check the timetable. If I leg it, I'll make the 10.25 a.m.

Everyone agrees that I need a holiday, that I'll feel better with a tan, that I should have a holiday fling. I try to explain that I don't do 'fling', I do serial monogamy. All my friends have real boyfriends (i.e., not the breed that run away days before you are due at the airport), and, therefore, none of them are available for said holiday. Undeterred, I did visit the travel agent. I'd argued to myself that it's a huge planet: surely there's a destination where it's possible – even acceptable – to be single and still get a suntan.

Apparently not.

For several excruciating minutes I discussed my travel plans with the woman behind the desk. She had big boobs, big bum, big hair and a big gob. I was feeling vulnerable. I noted that she had a huge diamond ring on her third finger, left hand. I didn't want to hate her because of this. So instead I hated her for making me admit, in public, that yes, I would have to pay the supplement for a single room. Since it's early July and I needed to depart immediately, my choices were limited. My financial state quickly reduced the choices from 'limited' to 'prohibitive'. I left the travel agent's more depressed than when I'd arrived. I walked in knowing I was sad, single and on the shelf. I left knowing that I'm also flat broke and flat-chested.

Well, you can't just mope at home . . .

I can.

You'll never meet Mr Right whilst watching *Gogglebox* . . .

Good point.

In the end, I was more or less forced to promise I'd visit seedy clubs, shag anything that moves and adopt a policy never to turn down an invitation.

The Brighton train leaves from platform 14. I'm getting to be quite an expert at working my way around Britain's stations. This is because I thought the answer to my holiday destination dilemma lay in a series of day trips. This week I have visited Bath, the Tower of London and Windsor Castle. All three proved to be edifying and educational trips. That is, if your idea of company is packs of schoolchildren – squalling and shrieking, it appears, is an international language – and if your idea of education is six-thousand-year histories potted into nine minutes of audiotape. My opportunities to buy souvenir tea towels and key rings have run into hundreds. My opportunities to flirt, fling or score: nil. Determined, I'm now trying Brighton.

I find an emptyish carriage and stare down a middle-aged woman and her son who were keen to bag the last couple of seats facing the direction of travel. The seat's mine; it's a small victory but it cheers me. I pass the journey staring out of the window watching the houses and fields rush by. I think this is symbolic.

Jen, I said symbolic, not 'some bollocks'. Anyway, what are you up to? . . . A survey of the world's hundred sexiest men. Really? Who wins? . . . Well, that's stupid. OK, I admit there is something interesting about Bradley Cooper, Jake Gyllenhaal and Idris Elba. But they are all too 'bad boy' to seriously consider for matrimony . . . Yes, Brad Pitt is marriage material but Angelina Jolie beat me to it . . . River Phoenix and James Dean are dead . . . I don't think including 'a young Sean Connery' is fair . . . Logan Lerman . . . Why are you laughing? Well, if it's not meant to be taken seriously, then what's the point of it? . . . Well, it doesn't make me feel sexy. Why would anyone want to do it *sur la plage*? To be honest, I've never watched the sun set on any part of a humping anatomy . . . I just can't imagine it in Brighton. It's not that there's anything wrong with Brighton per se. But it's not the Caribbean, is it? It's not even Ibiza . . . Yes, I'm sure it's very trendy now and a great place for a holiday fling . . . Yes, I know I've promised . . . Yes, I'll keep a lookout. I'll try. Got to go.

The train has just pulled up in Haywards Heath and my attention is caught by a group of blokes larking around on the platform. They are all in their mid twenties, therefore generally pretty spotty, but their overall impression is buoyed up by an overwhelming aura of self-confidence. There are five of them: one's ugly and happy-looking, two are average-looking but clean and trendy enough to push their score up to a six or seven out of ten. One is a clear eight, with all-American good looks. He might be interesting. The fifth has his back to me. My carriage pulls up parallel to where they are standing. I am stuck between willing them into my carriage – which is empty except for an old couple with a flask and egg sandwiches, and the disgruntled mother and son – and desperately wishing for them to sit elsewhere. The motivation for these opposing wishes is the same. If they sit nearby, the opportunities are ripe; this is 'fling alert'.

They choose my carriage. I bury my head in my book.

'Is this seat taken?'

I look up. Eleven out of ten. The most sensational-looking man *ever* is smiling at me. He is literally breathtaking. He is tall, with broad shoulders and slim hips. I wish he'd turn round so I can check out his bum properly. He has long, scruffy dark gypsy hair. It falls over his cobalt-blue eyes. He smiles. The smile ignites his entire face and many other parts of my body. I am too stunned to speak, and it takes all my presence of mind to shake my head. He sits down next to me. His knee brushes mine and my knickers jump into my throat.

'Going far?'

It's a simple enough question. I do know the answer but my tongue is temporarily paralysed. He stares at me strangely and then nods as if understanding something. He says slowly, 'Are. You. Going. All. The. Way?'

Now I am confused.

'To Brighton?' he adds.

I nod slowly.

'Where. Are. You. From?'

It's obvious from this that my stupid inability to answer his initial question has left him with the false impression that I am either deaf or foreign. Oh my God, how embarrassing. How do I put him straight? I think fast.

'Er, Paris,' I volunteer, but I pronounce it *'Oh, Pari.'*

'Je parle français.' He smiles.

Bugger, I don't. I got a D in my GCSE. Quick U-turn.

'But I em Swedeesh, not Paris.' I smile my newly acquired Swedish smile. He beams. And why wouldn't he? Show me a man who doesn't want to meet a Swede with a French education.

I soon discover that flirting is fun. Flirting in Swedish is doubly so. During the course of the journey I leave behind my British reserve and throw myself into my new persona. Unaccountably my hair is blonder, my breasts bigger and my thighs thinner. Or at least they must be, because Mick from Haywards Heath obviously finds me a super-babe. Then again, that could be because he is twenty-three.

A toy boy.

The idea is at once absurd and . . . attractive. I allow myself a few moments of respite from the particular breed of agony that is 'I am no longer Donald's woman' as I drift away into a fantasy of something other than a few quick thrusts. If I remember correctly, younger men do go long enough to guarantee a freight train shudder other than their own. My mum, my brother, Jen, Michelle and all my other friends are going to be so proud of me. Not only is this guy sex on legs, he's a toy boy, and since I have spent the last forty-five minutes making up a fictional persona for myself, including a new nationality, even I concede that this is not a relationship with a future. This is a fling.

For the last three months I have beaten the living daylights out of my Boots loyalty card in an attempt to defuzz, descale, retone and tan every inch of my body, which, thinking about it, is a not-so-bad-in-the-right-light-all-things-considered body. I have treated my credit cards with the same lack of respect as I assembled a beautiful wardrobe of tiny, flirty, pretty dresses and shoes.

And assuming that his entire cultural correspondence with Swedes is the same as mine – unfettered, uninhibited, up for it – Mick won't be able to resist. I know I'm right when two attractive women climb on to the train. His mates swoop but Mick doesn't seem to notice.

'Are you meeting anyone in Brighton?' asks Mick.

'I em alone.' I hope this makes me sound enigmatic rather than a loser. Mick grins again and I think I can safely assume it's the right answer. So far I haven't said much so he doesn't notice how phoney my accent is. He, on the other hand, has chatted freely. Assuming I understand little, he and his friends have discussed me openly; the only precaution they take is to speak quickly. I purposely misunderstand, interrupt in the wrong places and stare dumbly out of the window. I haven't had as much fun in ages.

'Check out the pert tits.'

Why thank you.

'Sensational.'

'Eesn't the view so?'

They stare at me, scared for a moment that I've understood.

'Sensational, the view.' I elaborate by waving at the window and they look relieved, nodding enthusiastically.

'Well, if you don't want her, mate, just say the word and I'll oblige.'

Excuse me!

'Forget it. She's gorgeous and I saw her first. Anyway, you're an ugly bastard and she wouldn't look at you.'

No, I wouldn't, but you, Mick, are certainly worth a second glance.

It's very hot and Brighton is heaving. Mick's mates walk all of two hundred yards from the station and suggest stopping for a drink. Mick and I make our excuses and tactically agree that we'll go on alone. I am flying. Helga (my pseudonym, for which I apologise; it shows a lack of imagination) has lent me a new-found confidence. I am open, misleading, worldly, guileless, arch and alluring by turn. It's easy because Helga manages to elicit cheap laughs by mispronouncing words and appearing charmed by kiss-me-quick hats and bubble gum machines. I can't remember a time when I wasn't trying to get married. Therefore my conversations with men are usually a thinly veiled attempt to check out their suitability. I mentally tick the lists. Right age, education and income bracket, evidence of ability to commit and ownership of a dog scores very highly for me. Helga doesn't want to get married – therefore, the deepest conversation Mick and I have is what type of topping we prefer on our crêpes. I'm in charge. I'm not trying to snare him. I can behave just as I please.

We wander through the Lanes, around the Pavilion and along the pier. Simultaneously we are both overcome with an enormous hunger. There are dozens of grotty cafés that serve strong tea in huge mugs with greasy chips and fried sausage. Normally I'm squeamish about cholesterol and I only eat nutritionally balanced, calorie-restricted meals. I don't think this caution is very Swedish, so I join Mick as he tucks into a gigantic fry-up.

Finally we make our way to the beach, which is pebbled rather than the white sands that I know Amelia will be treading. I don't hesitate but whip off my sundress. Mick nearly falls over as for a moment he thinks I've nothing but my birthday suit underneath. Even so, he doesn't look that disappointed with my bikini-clad bod. I can't believe I'm doing this. I'm normally so body-conscious I bathe with the lights out.

'Stones are better than sand, eh?' My accent is wavering monstrously. It would probably be better if I kept my mouth shut. Well, most of the time.

'Sorry?' asks Mick. I'm delighted to note that he isn't quite able to concentrate on what I'm saying.

'Sand it gets all where.' I elaborate. For the first time in a week I think I've got a better deal than Amelia. If I know anything about Donald's performance on holiday, sand is all Amelia will be getting in her knickers. Mick grins and I hope he is thinking what I'm thinking. He is.

'You are driving me wild,' he confirms, sitting down next to me on the pebbles.

'You want to go for, er, dive . . . er, drive?' I ask.

'No. Well, come to think of it . . .'

Of course I am not oblivious to my double entendre. I smile encouragingly.

'I said you are driving me wild,' he shouts. I continue to look confused but only so he has to repeat himself again. Each time he does, he raises his voice and I like the attention we are attracting. This is excellent news. I don't think I ever drove anyone wild when I held a British passport. With Donald it was definitely a case of familiarity breeding complacency. Towards the end we had settled into a routine of fortnightly sex, Donald's desire communicated to me by switching off the bedroom light and twiddling my nipple as though it were a radio dial.

Not that I'm considering having sex with Mick. I mean, I've only just met him. It would be indecent. It would be too forward. It would be risky.

It would be fun.

As a Swede, it's necessary to play the role to the full, i.e., be completely without reserve, hang-ups or shyness. I know I am pandering to stereotypes, but it is a once-in-a-lifetime opportunity to behave like a hussy without endangering the reputation of British girls. It's almost a patriotic act when I turn to him and push my tongue down his throat. He kisses me back. His kisses are expert; fiery, centred, exploratory. They last all afternoon. They last an age because we have nothing to say to each other. As this is a fling, I don't have to prove I'm intellectually stellar; I just have to be a tease. I run my hands up and down his body, checking out his taut muscles and lean waist.

'You are hard like a rock.' He blushes furiously and I know that I'm being childish, but it's the best fun I've had since . . . oh, I can't even remember when. Since I *was* a child, probably. His hands are dead still on my ribs, just millimetres from my breasts. My breasts are literally screaming for him to make his move. My nipples have stiffened and I hope to God that it's sweat I can feel between my legs. I'm demented.

The sun starts to set but the beach is still pretty busy. We watch people round up their cross kids; tired and burnt, they cry and argue with their siblings. Older couples are walking their dogs. They've already been back to their hotels; showered and changed into their pastel shirts and summer dresses. Whilst we watch them, they steadfastly try to avoid letting their gaze fall on us. I think they are afraid that our obvious lust and desire is infectious. I feel like shouting out and assuring them it's not. I should know. I've been trying to catch a bit of this long enough.

I shiver.

'Are you cold?'

'Before you say I am hot?' I feign confusion. He smiles and rubs his hands up and down my arms. It feels soooooo good. His fingers pierce me and yet his strokes are a balm. He caresses my ribs. They haven't made an appearance for years but are now sticking out everywhere. His hands weave around my breasts (despite my best efforts to get them to stop off there) and up to my shoulders and neck, which he massages firmly. I close my eyes and therefore feel rather than see him kiss my ears, which causes the hairs on my body to stand to attention. His fingers trace a route back down the side of my breasts, across my waist and over my stomach. Past the edge of my tiny bikini, where he wavers. Hesitating, hovering over all the areas that haven't got a suitable name. If he doesn't touch me soon, I'm going to combust.

I want this man to take me, to pull me, to push into me. I want this man. How do I broach the subject? Not easy in a first language; being Helga helps.

'Now we take 'otel?'

'Are you sure you want this?'

Want this? I want it more than I've ever wanted a wedding list at John Lewis.

Oh my God. Oh my God. Oh my God. Yes, it is me. Why do I sound different? . . . Yes, I am flung!! Well, at least Helga is . . . You heard. Who told you? . . . Liv. Saves me putting an announcement in the paper . . . Yes, Helga is a stupid name; I was under time pressure. The most amazing smile, sort of Bradley Cooper. Eyes to die for, kind of put me in mind of Zac Efron. The tightest butt, very Jake Gyllenhaal . . . His . . . Yes, huge! I seduced him with dinky little embroidered slip dresses and strappy sandals . . . Yes I know it takes two to tango . . . Sensational in bed and *sur la plage* . . . Well, you can't just mope at home . . . I really concede the point on flings. Thirties are great years . . . I'm freed from the insecurities that plagued my twenties . . . Sod the cellulite cream . . . After all, I am young, free and invited. No?

Round The Corner

She'd just dropped the kids off at her ex husband's. Tom was to have them for the entire weekend. How would she manage? Everyone said it'd be good to have time to herself, but she'd had most of the seven years she was married to herself. Tom was an absent father even when he lived with them. She was going to miss the kids' noise and clutter. Without them she wasn't sure she amounted to much at all.

She turned the corner and literally bumped into Shane – after all these years, there he was, sharing the same pavement. Some would call it fate; a coincidence at least. Leah believed in fate. It was fate that meant she'd got off work early and found Tom in bed with that woman. She'd worked for Sunitimes travel agency for eight years and her boss had never once said they could knock off early, until that day. Tom said he'd never brought another woman home, until that day. Not that she believed him. Fate often intervened when you least expected it; sometimes when you least wanted it.

It took a moment for them to place each other, but in the instant they did, Leah was seventeen again. She spun back in time and landed splat in his car, parked up outside her mum's house. She felt warm and safe. He looked older; well, she did too, naturally. But he smelt exactly the same. He smelt of her youth. As she leaned closer to secretly inhale him, she noticed he was trembling. She was too.

'You haven't changed a bit.' Shane grinned. The grin lit up her stomach and a bit lower, as it always had.

'Liar. Charmer but liar,' she laughed. 'Wow, it's been a long time.'

'Yes, fourteen years.' He paused and then added, 'Six months, one week.'

Delighted and shocked, Leah blushed. 'I don't believe you've been counting.'

'No, I haven't. I made up the stuff about months and weeks.' They both laughed again, forcing Leah to notice that she hadn't been doing much laughing lately.

'Fancy a drink?' he asked casually.

It was a no-brainer, as her son would say. They made their way to the nearest wine bar. She was impressed with the way he took charge, but it wasn't really her type of place. It was an intimidating, smart bar with trendy, wordless music playing loudly. She ordered a G&T; he had a beer. She asked for a double. She needed it. She didn't normally try to calm her nerves with drink. Then again, she wasn't normally nervous with men. She couldn't remember the last time she'd felt flirtatious or sexy. But she was nervous with Shane. And flirty. And sexy.

'So you don't drink Bacardi and Coke any more?' He smiled.

'No, and you've moved on from Woodpecker cider. Cheers.'

They clinked glasses, then fell silent, despite the fact that there was so much to say. Why hadn't he written after he went to university? Not a single reply to her letters? She remembered the futile, eternal waits for the postman. Truth was, he'd met a girl in Freshers' Week, and for the first two terms it seemed like love. He seemed to read Leah's mind. 'I never was much of a letter writer,' he said.

He wanted to ask her who she'd lost her virginity to, and was it good. The answer was that, furious and bored, she'd eventually had a fling with his cousin. Yes, it was good, very good. She read his mind too. 'Pretty average really,' she assured him. 'Like everyone's first time.'

They both started to laugh at the weird connection that seemed untroubled by the years of neglect. They'd always found talking easy, indulging in outpourings of opinions and dreams. That much hadn't changed. She told him about Tom. The ink was barely dry on the decree absolute; still raw, her tale needed retelling.

'Dozy devil,' said Shane dismissively.

'For getting caught?'

'For letting you go.' He looked right at her and she felt his gaze splinter in her stomach.

'*You* did.'

'I'm a dozy devil too. Biggest mistake of my life.'

She laughed. He might be flattering her, he might be serious. In that moment it didn't matter. A tiny piece of discontent and disappointment dissolved inside her, and she breathed a little easier. It would do to believe him, at least for now, and maybe longer.

'What are you up to this weekend?' he asked.

'Nothing much.'

'Fancy going to the movies?'

'I haven't been to the cinema for years; well, aside from kids' films.'

'I'll stretch to popcorn. Fizzy pop?'

She'd thought it was impossible to feel seventeen unless you *were* seventeen, but now with Shane, it was back, that overwhelming sense of possibility.

'OK.'

The past was just that, but new beginnings were around every corner.

It's A Dog's Life

'I suggest you pick yourself up and get out there immediately. You're not a teenager.'

'Thanks for that, Mum,' I say sarcastically. 'But I don't feel like going anywhere.'

'You won't meet anyone sitting watching TV,' she scolds. 'I always thought Aiden had shifty eyes.' True, she'd said so many times before.

Jasmine from work seduced him with her scary power suits and whizzy PowerPoint presentations. He was forever complaining that I lacked ambition and was covered in dog hair. I paint portraits of dogs; mostly from photographs, but if the sitter allows it, I sometimes paint live. I don't earn much, but I love my work. How many people can say that?

Hector, my stalwart, adorable mutt, pads towards me. He brushes up against my legs, tail wagging slowly but purposefully, then he settles at my feet; I can feel the warmth of his body. Call me crazy, but his expression says he sympathises. I blow my nose and ram another chocolate into my mouth.

'You don't want to turn into one of those lonely old spinsters with no one in her life other than her pet,' says Mum.

'Wouldn't bother me. At least I'm the only woman in Hector's life. I don't have to worry that if he gets off his lead he's up to anything more than chasing cats. He doesn't come home reeking of another woman's perfume and he doesn't tell me lies. Hector is a loyal boy.'

My mother sighs. She doesn't understand my love for Hector and all things canine. When I was a kid, I had to content myself with plastering my walls with posters of adorable floppy puppies and independent sleek mutts. The minute I got my own place, I adopted Hector from the RSPCA. He's been by my side for eleven years now; whereas Luc, Aran, Will, Nick, etc. have come and gone. Now Aiden has gone too.

I gently rub behind Hector's ears. He nuzzles his wet nose into my hand reassuringly.

I work from home, which Hector loves. We keep each other company. Whilst I paint, he sits on the floor by the windowsill of my studio (a rather grandiose name for the box spare room). He only wakes up and nudges my hand to tell me it's lunchtime or that he needs a run. Mostly, I'm disciplined about his exercise. I enjoy walking him in the nearby park; however, if I get very caught up with what I'm working on, I admit to lazily opening the door and allowing him to charge around the communal gardens. None of my neighbours can object because at the end of the day I always dash about with a pocketful of plastic bags, just to check that Hector hasn't left any unwanted surprises behind.

That's why it is unusual that on Monday he stays out all morning, only coming in from the communal gardens after I've called for him for a good five minutes; he's normally so obedient. Then on Tuesday and Wednesday, straight after breakfast, he starts to whine and scratch at the door. I only remember lunch when my stomach rumbles. When he is home he seems pre-occupied and shows no interest in his toys. By Friday I'm really worried because he doesn't even want to snuggle up with me and watch TV.

I call Sara for advice. She's my best friend and mum to three dogs and two cats; she's very experienced.

'Maybe he's missing Aiden.'

'Not possible. They didn't really get on.' I'm adamant.

'Are you crying a lot? You might be upsetting him.'

'I've cried a bit,' I admit reluctantly. 'We were together nine months, and as my mum never tires of pointing out, I'm not getting any younger. I'd thought Aiden might be the One.'

'Even though Hector didn't like him?'

'Good point,' I concede. Hector's a good judge of character so I tried to ignore his sullen apathy towards Aiden – and all my other boyfriends, come to that. Oddly, I've never dated what you'd call a dog lover.

Over the following fortnight, I become increasingly distraught as Hector's indifference towards me develops into something that might be interpreted as dislike. He won't eat anything I offer, although our vet says he isn't ailing (he hasn't lost any weight). He stays away from home for increasingly lengthy periods, and when he is home, he stalks the floor between me and the front door, making it clear he'd rather be elsewhere.

'Sounds like he's moving on,' says Sara sadly. "That's how we got Sugar Plum. She started visiting us regularly and eating from our cats' bowls.'

'But Sugar Plum is a cat, not a dog. Dogs are known for their loyalty and cats are not.' I try not to sound huffy, but what she's suggesting is offensive. Sara does seem to care but calmly carries on with her explanation and theory.

'In the end I had to discuss the situation with our neighbour. It transpired they'd just had twin babies. Sugar Plum was fed up.'

'But I don't have twins!' I yell.

'Something is upsetting him.'

The next morning Hector whines at the door for a good twenty minutes, I reach for his lead but as I open the door he scrambles away from my grip before I can harness him. Dashing, I follow him outside. Gutted, I watch as he runs straight into a house across the road.

Incensed, I bang on the door. Whoever this hussy is, I'm going to have it out with her. I stood by and allowed Jasmine to move in on Aiden, but Hector means more to me. I'm going to fight for him.

The door swings open and a man, rather than a woman, answers.

'You have my dog,' I screech.

'Sorry?' He looks bewildered. He's also handsome, with eyes that sparkle brighter than Hector's, but I'm not going to be distracted. This dog thief can't divert me just by being gorgeous.

'Hector is mine and you have no right luring him away. I bet you feed him bacon and chocolates.'

'No, no, not at all. I'm Oli.' He holds out a hand for me to shake.

I ignore it. 'That's not an appropriate diet for—'

'Whoa, slow down.'

'You can't have him. He's mine!' I yell, refusing to be soothed by his reasonable tone.

'I have no intention of stealing your dog.'

'I love him. We belong together.'

'He seemed lonely. *He* approached me.'

'He's all I've got.'

Suddenly there's silence. Hector has come to the door to see what all the fuss is about. He looks at me with what I take to be embarrassment. Oli looks embarrassed too. What made me confess such a thing?

'I'm sorry to hear that.' He pauses. It seems we are both lost for words. 'I'm not trying to steal your dog. I have two of my own.'

'You're a dog lover?'

'Would you like to meet them?'

I look at Hector. He's circling Oli's legs and I swear he's pleading with me to accept. I nod and follow Oli to the kitchen. As I settle on to a stool at the breakfast bar, I suddenly get the feeling that it's all going to be OK, and that Hector will be persuaded to come home with me, after the coffee.

'You cheeky little matchmaker,' I whisper into his silky ear.

I swear he winks at me.

Wake-Up Call

I can't imagine why I'm here. What possessed me to accept an invite to a college reunion? When the envelope dropped on to my doormat, my first reaction was to put it in the bin. Why would I want to meet up with people I haven't seen for years? Surely, the point is, if we'd wanted to stay in touch we would have.

I graduated eight years ago, and despite popular myth, student years were not the best years of my life. I remember them as a blur of damp accommodation, cheap curries, a series of broken hearts and essay crises. Whilst I send Christmas cards to about half a dozen old acquaintances, I only really have three true friends from college. One of whom lives in Australia and does something impressive as a management consultant. Another lives in India and does something worthy in a hospital in the Calcutta slums. And Laura. Laura works as a junior copywriter in a small advertising agency but dreams of writing novels. I am a temp receptionist on my third career break and I dream about a knight in shining amour.

We share a flat, and it was Laura who insisted that I attend this reunion.

'You can't not,' she argued. 'What else will you be doing that night?'

Which seemed to settle it.

We push open the bar door and I'm hit by the smell of beer-soaked carpets. Laura starts waving to people. I don't actively recognise anyone, although one or two faces are vaguely familiar. We force our way to the bar and buy a bottle of wine. That's my idea, because if we find a table we can offer people a drink when they join us, and they are more likely to join us if they see there's a chance of a free drink. It's not that I'm lacking in confidence per se, but tonight I feel about as sparkly as a cheap bottle of cider that was opened last week. Laura, on the other hand, is bouncing. She's insisting on smiling at everyone and she even thinks the name tags are a good idea. Mine's spelt wrong.

'It is you, isn't it?' I recognise Anna Crompton's voice without having to check the tag.

'Wow, Anna, you look wonderful,' says Laura, flinging her arms around her. Anna smiles, and although she shoots a glance up and down both Laura and me, she doesn't return the compliment. I pass the bottle of Chardonnay and an empty glass and pray for the evening to be over.

'Are you married?' she asks, with all the subtlety of lacy red underwear. Our silence is our confession. Neither Laura nor I are even regularly dating, which suits Laura and horrifies me.

'I got married last summer,' smiles Anna. Which I suppose explains why she's here. She never was one for team events, but she obviously saw this as a good opportunity to gloat. Her recently married state also explains why she is glowing. I try not to resent it.

'Have you seen Jess?' she asks as she looks around the bar. Anna, Laura, Jess and I were not only in the same hall of residence, but we also all did the same course. This should mean we have plenty in common.

'There she is,' says Laura, pointing excitedly towards the door.

Jess waves, blows kisses, and then flies towards us. She oozes activity. She always did. She is one of those people who always has thousands of friends to see and places to go. I lost touch with Anna because she's a horror to be with; I lost touch with Jess because I didn't have the energy to keep up.

Jess is still striking. If I'm pedantic and draw a distinction between beautiful and attractive, then she's attractive – but quite especially so. She's wearing her hair in a silky bob. Her face is always exquisite: enormous brown eyes framed with Bambi lashes, a wide nose and a lopsided rose-red mouth.

Everyone air-kisses everyone else and then we settle down.

'I hear you're married now, eh?' says Jess, nudging Anna.

This is all the prompting Anna needs. From nowhere she produces wedding photos and starts to give us a blow-by-blow account from first kiss onwards. I remember when she wasn't above going out and getting wrecked, losing her shoes and, if not quite flashing her boobs at passers-by, then at least insisting she could pee standing up. Now, it appears, all she can talk about is matching towels from M&S and the importance of damp-proofing.

It's so depressing.

And what's more depressing is that I'd pay a king's ransom to be so blissfully content with domestic dreariness, which makes me ashamed that women chained themselves to railings for me and, worse yet, burnt good underwear.

Laura entertains us with stories about the advertising agency and details her plans for getting her novel published. She's been thwarted on a number of occasions: she regularly receives don't-call-us-we'll-call-you letters from publishing houses and agents. She puts this down to their inability to take risks. One thing that can be said for Laura: she certainly isn't a quitter. I drift off as I look out of the window. The sun is doing its best – not exactly shining, more shimmering from time to time, whenever there's a gap in the clouds. I must have drunk too much: I'm feeling maudlin.

'What's up?' asks Laura.

I'm that transparent. I shrug.

'How's the teaching going?' asks Jess politely.

'Teaching?' I'm confused.

'Didn't you always want to be a teacher?'

God, I'd almost forgotten wanting that. 'Er, never panned out. Couldn't face more exams after I got my degree.'

'Oh.' Jess nods but she doesn't ask what I do instead.

'Are you seeing anyone at the moment?' asks Anna, but only because she knows the answer.

'I was seeing a lawyer until quite recently,' I tell her. 'Didn't work out.'

'Why not?'

I shrug again. The trouble is, it's difficult for me to explain exactly what went wrong. The problems, which must have been obvious to him, are indefinable to me. He said he wanted us to finish. That's all he said. Odd, because I'd spent my morning planning mini breaks in Edinburgh or Prague – somewhere cold, so we'd have to cuddle; somewhere old, so I could pretend to be cultured.

I asked him if he thought things were moving too quickly or if he thought I was commitment-shy. I offered him a range of options, from large white wedding to let's just be friends. He didn't comment. We had the most silent break-up *ever*. I can't see him making much of a living as a barrister. His silence was particularly frustrating because when I met him I was almost overwhelmed by how very interesting, articulate and clever he was. He had an opinion on just about every subject you can imagine and it *always* impresses and thrills me when people can talk knowledgeably about climate change, politics, history, sport – any or a combination. All I can talk about with any certainty is feelings.

Laura always maintained that the lawyer was a bit overly fond of his own voice, but then she thought the management consultant was too materialistic, the web designer too flighty, the estate agent too manic. Tinker, tailor, soldier, sailor, none of them ever meets her criteria. I think she's too picky. She thinks I'm not picky enough. She's always saying I deserve better, if only I could see that. I tell her the issue is getting other people – male people – to see me at all; that's challenge enough. She usually sighs at this point in the discussion and offers to make a cup of tea.

I wonder if the girls can throw any light on the break-up. I reach for the wine and pour myself a generous glass.

'I know it's mostly my pride that's bruised. He was nice enough, but . . .' I leave the sentence unfinished. Nice enough is condemnation enough.

'Just physical, then? Good sex?' asks Jess.

'Not even that.'

We grin. I decide against telling her that I can't remember when I last had good sex. The most I hope for nowadays is an absence of any out-and-out peculiarities: an over-reliance on sex toys, premature ejaculation, ingrowing toenails, hairy back . . .

'How's Dave?'

Dave is Jess's husband. They met during Freshers' Week and have been together ever since. Thirteen years! The longest relationship I've ever had is four and a half months. Unless you count Karl, but you can't really count Karl as that only lasted two years because he lives in Germany.

'Fine.' She hesitates and then adds, 'I imagine.'

She quickly reaches for the wine bottle, tuts when she sees it's empty and bangs it back down on to the table. There is so obviously something wrong that you can almost touch it in the air.

Finally she says, 'We're getting divorced.'

'Divorced?' repeats Laura with astonishment.

'Did he have an affair?' asks Anna angrily.

I'm too stunned to say anything. Jess shakes her head. She's obviously debating whether old friendships that have been neglected are still relevant. It could be the distance between us that prompts her to go on.

'Nobody warned me. Nobody told me the important stuff, like why don't respect, peace and trust always add up to being in love? How can we possibly have mistaken excitement, passion and lust for love?'

'*You* had an affair,' says Laura, deadpan.

Jess nods and puts her head on the table. Her silky hair falls forward into a puddle of wine. She doesn't seem to notice, or if she does, she doesn't care. I'm fascinated and repelled.

Our intimate party breaks up fairly swiftly after that. Some blokes who studied geography ask if they can join our table, and instead of shunning these nerds as we always did in the old days, we welcome them eagerly. None of us wants to face the intensity of Jess's confession. We drink a lot and then drunkenly swap telephone numbers, promising to not leave it as long next time.

Laura and I treat ourselves to a cab home.

'You're quiet. Did you hate it?' she asks.

'I'm glad I went.'

'What, even though your dream of happily-ever-after was blown apart when you heard Jess's news?'

'Especially because of that.'

Laura starts to chat about how grey someone-or-other is and how wrinkled thingy-me-bobby is but how radiant blah-blah is. I barely follow. My mind is full of plans. I don't say so, but I plan to get up really early tomorrow morning and get on the internet to research teacher training places. Because while it might just be the alcohol giving me a false sense of optimism and a new perspective, I don't think it is. Jess's story, and Anna's too, for that matter, didn't depress me as I'd have expected; they poked and prodded me. Never again will I sit in a room and admit that my only news is that a mute barrister has ditched me. Even a divorce seems more of an achievement than doing nothing at all.

'You didn't mean it when you said we should meet up again, did you?' asks Laura.

'I might have. I think I did.' Laura looks surprised but pleased. 'The thing is, Laura, life is what passes you by when you are waiting for something to happen.'

Laura looks confused. 'Did you read that on a Hallmark card?'

'Probably, but it doesn't mean it's not profound.' She looks sceptical so I admit, 'Well, it probably does, but either way I've decided not to wait any longer.'

She doesn't understand but she puts her arm around me anyway. She'll get it. I'll show her. I'll show myself.

Adele Shares . . .

What I Never Travel Without

I find packing for my holidays horribly traumatic. It's almost hideous enough to make me not want to go on holiday at all. I'm prone to a tiny bit of exaggeration, but I feel I'm not over-stating that. The thing is no matter how hard I try it seems that I never, ever pack what I need, even though I often have to pay excess baggage as I seem to pack everything I own! How can that be? I just don't understand – it's like a modern mystery akin to the existence or not of the Loch Ness monster. I know I'm supposed to pack 'lite'; I've read as much in all the beautiful, glossy magazines that promise a beautiful, glossy life. Packing 'lite' is what stylish, accomplished, in-control types do; they have capsule wardrobes. However, packing 'lite' bothers me on two levels:

1. It is impossible
2. It is invariably spelt incorrectly

The reality is that toiletries weigh a tonne and, as my holiday is the only time of year it actually matters to me whether I smear cellulite prevention/harnessing/cure cream all over my body, then toiletries have to feature. (I do realise that the cellulite cream is unlikely to work in the fortnight I'm in the sun and I should have started a regime in January but I'm never that organised, ho hum). Fact, I am no longer twenty-five; a slick of sun cream and a bit of mascara alone does not cut it. I need to pack full make-up, de-frizzing shampoo and conditioner (oh, the humidity!), serums, sun cream, a body brush, fake-tan, exfoliators, moisturisers (for my face, neck, legs, bot, belly) – you name it, I need it! Hair straighteners *and* curlers *and* hairdryer all have to come with me because, basically, I look nothing like my promo pics in real life. In real life I'm much more . . . unkempt. Most of the time this bothers me not a jot because I'm rarely seen (writers can hide behind their computers for long stretches of the year), but when it comes to holidays I suddenly feel an overwhelming desire/ craving/pressure to be as glam as I can be. The result is, my case is already half full and I haven't even thought about clothes . . .

I watch as my husband tosses a few T-shirts, a pair of trousers, a pair of swimmers and some shorts into a case. He zips it closed with a flourish and throws out a slightly annoying grin that tells me he thinks summer packing is easy-peasy. I know he'll look great the entire holiday; he'll be absolutely, suitably clad on all occasions and will not be caught red and sweating or blue and shivering.

I try to ape him but here's the thing: besides the basics that he's packed I also need vest tops, dresses (day and evening), underwear (lavish and functional) skirts and shirts, plus is it costume or bikini and how many of each? Whilst unearthing my carefully secreted summer clothes from the plastic drawer under my bed, I find that my heart sinks a little rather than takes flight. I always think I have loads of summer clothes but every time it comes to packing (which is usually a rush job the night before we fly) I discover that apparently the previous summer I thought boobtubes, floral rah-rah skirts, and neon pedal-pushers were a good idea. Looking down at my garish, flimsy summer clothes with slight despair, I wonder whether the rare dose of sunshine shocks me so severely it causes a temporary loss of sanity. It's possible because it seems that each summer I suffer from severe colour blindness and an inability to estimate dress size (manifesting in brassy, gaudy, far too tight numbers). Still, time is ticking and so I throw everything that's even vaguely summery into my case.

Then there are shoes. Now, I hold my hands up here. I do own a lot of shoes. Approximately 40 pairs, plus 20 trainers, 15 sandals, 10 boots and 5 flip-flops. I have only two feet. Clearly, the maths doesn't work. I rarely throw out footwear because I tell myself that they'll come back into fashion and have one more day to shine. Glancing at my racks of shoes is a little like flicking through a photo album – I always let out an involuntary gasp of excitement. My shoes harbour memories; they conjure a sense of overwhelming sentimentality and joy and have all the potency, secrecy and illicit pleasure of a diary. I want to pack them all – OK, well, maybe not the boots, but all the others. My husband scowls, huffs and puffs so in the end I limit myself to one pair of trainers, one pair of flip flops and one set of heels. A decision I bitterly regret every moment of my holiday!

Finally, just before I force the zip, I fling in a floppy hat, a sun cap, sarongs, insect repellent, antiseptic cream, plasters, handbags, jewellery, five or six books and a few more T-shirts, just in case . . .

Each year I vow I will be more organised, ruthless, realistic and that I'll make a better job of packing. Each year I fail. It doesn't matter though because once I'm abroad, prone and soaking up the sun, I find that all I really need is a beach towel, a bikini and a book.

Let me know what has to go on holiday with you!
@adeleparks #LoveIsAJourney

HAPPY ENDINGS

Besotted

Was this it? Was this what it all amounted to?

All that effort. Those endless yearnings, those fragile hopes, those passionate declarations; was this where it all ground to a halt? Makala sighed, but her disappointment was inaudible above the blaring TV, where some skinny pop princess was animatedly running through the rules of the latest celebrity reality humiliation-fest.

Makala had always been a romantic. Aged ten, she started writing boys' names on her pencil case, framing those names with fat inky hearts and wild imaginings. Then there were the telephone years, when she received and made countless calls and sent flirty texts to spotty and sporty guys who smelt of vivid hormones. In her twenties she'd had endless hot and not-so-hot dates; she'd sat in restaurants, pubs, bars, at parties, ice rinks, cinemas and bowling alleys as she relentlessly pursued the quest to find her One.

During this time it transpired that Makala was a woman with whom it was easy to fall in and out of love. She expected a lot from life, from the people she shared her time with and from herself. This made her exhilarating and exasperating at the same time. Many mattresses had creaked as she'd opened her heart and her legs to the possibilities. Makala didn't regret a single kiss; every one of them had been a journey. Admittedly, some were more like bus rides to the local job centre, but they were bearable because a few were flights to exotic and memorable places and you just never knew which kiss was going to be what sort of journey.

And then there was Ben. Ben, who blew all the other guys out of her head and her bed. Ben, who she ran down the aisle with. Her One.

Makala took a sneaky sideways glance at her husband at the same time as she reached for another sweet out of the tin that sat between them. Only the hard-centre chocs were left. They'd languished there for a couple of nights now, beneath notice. But Makala was desperate; she needed something sweet to help her swallow what they had become. She stuffed the toffee into her mouth, chewed and considered.

She did not fancy him. Not any more. How could it be possible to fancy a man who had just raised his butt cheek (the one nearest her) and let out a gentle *phut* sound? He didn't even bother to excuse himself, or in any way acknowledge that she was in the room and therefore subject to his bodily functions. She had merged into the wallpaper. His stomach rolled over his belt. He wasn't enormous; he didn't need help getting up and down the stairs – he was some way from that just yet – but he was distinctly chubby. Plump enough that if he was a girl, he'd feel self-conscious when having a cuddle or his photo taken. His roll of fat was the direct result of too many comfy couple meals and takeaways in front of the TV. He needed a shave and new clothes too. All of this she could forgive, easily, if only he still saw her. Noticed her. Like he used to.

Makala had to admit she wasn't exactly a supermodel herself. Since Christmas she had eaten her body weight in Quality Street. She'd bought one of those big family tins, designed for sharing, but they'd never got round to inviting people over so they'd consumed the lot between them. At first like hungry locusts, swooping down on the purple ones with a whole hazelnut in soft, luscious caramel, and the orange-flavoured truffle with crunchy bits; but now more like stuffed sloths, still somehow managing to force more chocolate down their gullets. Perhaps they both knew it saved them from conversation.

'Is there anything else on?' Makala asked. Silence. She waited a reasonable length of time in order to establish whether Ben had heard her and was simply considering his response or whether he had no intention of replying, perhaps now totally deaf to her tones. When it became apparent he wasn't planning on speaking, she asked again. 'Is this all that's on?'

'Eh?'

'TV? Is this all that's on TV?'

They had Sky Movies, Sky Sports, Sky Plus . . . Sky Repeats. A choice of several million channels, minimum; surely there was something more edifying than this. Makala glanced at the TV and watched in horror as an ancient has-been kids' TV presenter licked ice cream off the body of an ex never-quite-been glamour girl. Never-quite-been because the glamour girl had in fact been a glamorous guy until he'd had the op. Makala was disappointed with herself for knowing this piece of trivia, but she found that however much she wanted to avoid the realities of the trashy culture she lived amongst, it seeped into her consciousness by a process of osmosis.

Ben slowly picked up the remote and began to switch between channels. In amongst the deadening array of repeats and reality shows Makala caught a glimpse of a costume drama clinch. Momentarily she shuddered with excitement at the thought of a couple of hours vicariously enjoying someone else's romance, passion and smouldering looks; she didn't care if the romance was historical, fictional or even badly acted. But she didn't get opportunity to dwell as Ben continued to rotate through the channels and simply commented, 'Load of crap.'

And she had to agree with him.

It was.

It *all* was.

Makala blamed her parents. The name they had given her was far too pretty and unusual for the life she'd been born into. Hers wasn't an awful life, she realised that. She was very fortunate in many ways. She was able-bodied, born into the free world in the twenty-first century, where hot and cold running cappuccinos and frappés were freely available on every street corner. She and Ben were well enough off. Not millionaires, but they lived in a nice two-bedroom semi. A great little starter home, her dad called it. They could always pop out for a meal on a Friday night, order more wine than sensible, tip heavily and not have to worry about their bank card being rejected. Not that they did pop out on a Friday night very often any more. They didn't pop or even amble anywhere. Ben was as devoid of drive as a ride-on lawnmower.

Recently Makala had begun to worry that her starter home would be her finisher home too. Would she be carried out of this place in a wooden box in sixty years, with nothing more to show for her life than a clutch of photos of grandkids and maybe a jar of kidney stones that her surgeon had thought she might like to keep? Her life was a very normal one, and whilst she felt ungrateful that she wasn't more excited by it, she could not help but regret that it was not the romantic one she had dreamed of and expected, somehow, to graduate into once she was past her mid twenties. It was a problem. Makala was the name of an exotic heroine, not an office administrator who worked for a second-rate solicitor in a mid-size town in the Midlands. And Ben (Benedict, actually) was definitely the name of a romantic hero – someone comfortable in breeches, and yet still manly – not a man who worked in a large IT consultancy and whose idea of romance was taking the cap off the beer bottle before he handed it to his wife.

Makala sighed and looked around for amusement beyond Ben and the box that had become his baby. Not a box, actually; a box suggested chubby and substantial. Their TV was a sleek forty-eight-inch flat screen. Ben loved it as much as Makala loathed it. Its very sleekness seemed to somehow contrast unfavourably with her ever-expanding waistline and cellulite-puckered thighs. Princess Diana might have thought *her* marriage was crowded, but at least there was some seemliness, or at least precedent, in being replaced by another woman; being replaced by a TV was simply humiliating.

Makala knew she was beginning to get hysterical; she was prone to this. It was her romantic nature. She needed to call her girlfriends for a chat; they would help her remain reasonable and rational, or at the very least would amuse her more than watching the glamour girl covered in ice cream.

Makala and her mates used to meet in Dylan's, the cocktail bar on Market Street, every Friday night; they'd drink margaritas in the summer and red wine or Manhattans in the winter. They'd dress up in skirts and heels – sort of Brummie Carrie Bradshaws – and for short chunks of time would be impossibly glamorous and frivolous. But for one reason or another those girlie evenings didn't happen so often nowadays, and Makala missed them.

Karen had two babies now. It defied logic, but after approximately fifteen years of responsible use of contraception, she had apparently lost the knack. She fell pregnant on her honeymoon, and no sooner had she remembered why she was constantly bothering to do her pelvic floor exercises than she fell pregnant again. Karen had, through necessity, downgraded her idea of glamour to managing to get to Tumble Tots without spew on her coat.

Lizzie was newly engaged and too busy at dress fittings to make time to drink cocktails; besides, she had turned all nil-by-mouth since her engagement so wasn't much fun on a bender, as she could (and would) tell you exactly how many calories there were in any drink on the menu.

Devi was still feverishly hunting for her One and seemed to be endlessly on a trail of dinner, lunch, brunch, blind, speed and internet dates. She constantly grumbled that there were no decent men out there, but Makala couldn't help but notice that Devi seemed to be having so much damn fun looking. Makala didn't like to dwell, but being around Devi left her feeling . . . what was it? Dissatisfied? Curious? Jealous?

Hell.

In the absence of a decent evening of gossip and giggles, she made do with using up her free minutes on her mobile. She called Karen first. Having waited until after 9 p.m., she had hoped for a conversation that wouldn't be constantly interrupted by Karen talking to the children or, worse still, putting them on the phone so that Makala could listen as they gurgled nonsensically. OK, she was the eldest one's godmother, but really only the actual birth mother of a child could be interested in the sound of their la-la-ing.

'Did you get nice gifts?' asked Karen. She was trying to sound breezy but her words were slurred. Makala deduced that she had already downed the best part of a bottle of wine, no doubt celebrating the fact that both children were asleep at the same time – a rare occurrence. Makala knew that Karen's tolerance to alcohol had been lowered due to nearly two years of breastfeeding; she had about thirty minutes before Karen passed out, so she spoke quickly.

'Christmas gifts were predictable. A new coat. It's lovely; I picked it out myself from the Next catalogue.'

'Lucky you.'

Oddly, Karen didn't sound facetious but Makala was sure she must be being so. Makala had wanted frilly Agent Provocateur underwear, Prestat champagne truffles in a pretty pink box and sensuous Molton Brown bath oil. The sort of gifts featured in Sunday supplement gift suggestion guides from mid October onwards. The sort of gifts that suggested a sexy, alluring, thrilling lover and lifestyle. Ben hadn't so much as bought her a selection box of his own volition.

'What about you?' Makala asked dutifully.

'Oh, we didn't bother with gifts for one another this year. We have the kids to buy for. There doesn't seem much point.'

Karen then went on to detail a million toys all with different bells and whistles that she and Mick had bought their children. It appeared that Karen had all but disappeared under a mountain of Lamaze rattles, cloth books, soft toys and twelve-piece jigsaws. Makala found it difficult to keep track of the pros and cons of VTech, Leapfrog and Tomy; they were all plastic. She hadn't thought it was possible to feel more irritated and bored than when she was sitting in front of the TV with Ben, but hey-ho, who knew. She sighed rudely. Karen either wilfully or tactfully chose to interpret the sigh as one of frustration rather than incivility.

'You should get pregnant; that eliminates the possibility of any introspection,' she said, entirely as though she thought it was a good thing.

Makala made her excuses to hang up and called Lizzie instead.

'Happy New Year,' trilled Lizzie.

'Thanks, and you. What did you get up to?'

'We went to the most amazing party. At the King's Hotel.' Makala's ears pricked up. She loved the King's Hotel. It was really classy. Unquestionably the nicest place to stay in a thirty-mile radius of their town. She deeply regretted that the year she and Ben got married it was being refurbished.

'We are definitely going to have the wedding reception there,' said Lizzie. She always referred to her wedding as *the* wedding.

'You should have said you were going there. Ben and I would have come along too,' said Makala, resentfully remembering her own New Year's Eve. They'd stayed at her in-laws', eating saturated-fat leftovers until midnight, when they'd watched the fireworks in London on the TV. The irony that sparks were going off elsewhere wasn't lost on Makala: she and Ben had been in bed by twenty past twelve; he was asleep by twenty-two minutes past.

'It was invitation only,' replied Lizzie, not quite managing to keep the smugness out of her voice. 'Just for couples who had registered an interest in getting married there this year. The waiters were dressed as groomsmen and the waitresses as bridesmaids. The tables looked divine, the flowers, the glassware . . .'

Makala remembered being equally excited about planning her own wedding. Now that seemed unbelievable. She confessed as much to Lizzie.

'What do you mean?' asked Lizzie, shocked into uttering an entire sentence that had no mention of tulle or buttonholes.

'I remember that feeling of complete absorption in the wedding, in Ben, in our lives, but I can't recapture it.'

'Oh my God!'

'I know.'

'But you're happy, right?' Lizzie needed to hear this reassurance as much for herself as for her friend; she must have doubted she was going to get it as she rushed on. 'I mean, Ben's great, isn't he? He's your Mr Right. He's the man who goes out to buy you chocolate and *Heat* magazine when you have period pains; he's the man who introduced you to fried egg sandwiches.' Just when Makala was beginning to worry that all of Ben's seduction skills were food-related, Lizzie added, 'The man who sat through *Hamlet* because you have a crush on David Tennant. He took you to the Maldives for your thirtieth. You *have* to be happy.'

Makala couldn't quite bring herself to agree that she was actually happy, not at this precise moment of time – she was thirty-three now, and her tan from the Maldives had well and truly faded – so she said nothing. It wasn't as though she needed endless holidays – that wasn't what she meant – but a bit of conversation might go some way towards increased happiness.

After a while Lizzie asked, 'What is it you want, Makala?'

Makala wanted butterflies' wings beating in her stomach, a springing in her knickers when she thought of him, a giddiness in her heart and a dizziness in her head. She wanted him to be besotted, her to be fanatical; she wanted it all.

'You should go sale-shopping,' suggested Lizzie.

Makala called Devi. But Devi had the least time of all to chat, as she was changing the sheets in between dates.

'You are kidding, right?' asked Makala, trying not to sound like the prude she felt she was.

Devi giggled. 'What can I tell you? I'm dating two hot guys. Neither of them has asked for any exclusivity and I don't feel ready to commit either – I'm having too much fun.'

'Don't. You're making me feel terrible. I'm so bored I think I'm dead.'

'Do something about it.'

'Like what? Karen said I should have a baby, Lizzie suggested I sale-shop.'

'You could have an affair.'

'Ha ha.'

'I'm serious.'

'I'm not the type.'

'Everyone is the type,' Devi said darkly.

'You're no bloody help. I'm going to go and have a long bath now. Wash away your foul and dirty joke,' replied Makala sardonically. Devi *was* joking, right? 'Maybe we can go out next week?' she added, not actually expecting it to happen.

'I'll check my diary. Good idea about the bath, though. Do you have candles? Don't forget soft music. You go and give yourself a lovely big orgasm and you'll feel much better.'

'You're disgusting. You know I don't see the point in masturbation and I never do it.'

'Well, you should. It's fun. Being naughty is fun.' Devi hung up.

It started in February. The fifth, a Thursday. Makala took care to ring Ben to say that she would be late home.

'Girls' night out,' he asserted, rather than asked. Of course it was a girls' night out, why else would Makala be late home; she wasn't the type to work extra hours. Ben didn't even notice that she hesitated momentarily before agreeing with him. It was just an infinitesimal moment in time. It was utterly decisive.

He was a bit surprised when she arranged to meet up with Devi on Valentine's night, a Saturday. Not that he had planned anything especially for Valentine's night. He thought the entire day was a load of commercially driven bollocks and made it a point of principle not to buy a card, but normally Makala insisted they share a bottle of champagne. Makala explained that Devi was struggling because Valentine's night was the most feared date in a single girl's diary.

'But didn't you say she's dating two blokes at the moment?' asked Ben.

'Did I?' Makala was taken aback that Ben had remembered this detail; he hadn't taken his eyes off the TV when she relayed the intricacies of Devi's sexual conquests, and she'd assumed he wasn't listening. 'Yeah, erm, she is. That's the problem. If she sees one of them she's sort of committing to something serious, and she's not ready for that.'

'I thought men were traditionally the commitment-shy ones.'

'Outdated stereotype. Women like sex for sex's sake too, you know,' snapped Makala.

The next three Thursdays in a row Makala met up with her friends, or so Ben assumed. He didn't actually ask. He was never awake when she got home and he wasn't a morning sort of person so he didn't like to chat over his cornflakes. What was the point of asking anyway? Her girls' nights out were always the same, always would be: gossipy, tipsy and late.

On Thursday 5 March Makala announced that she was going to a book signing in town for World Book Day or something, whatever the hell that was. She had never been to a book signing before but Ben didn't doubt that this was what she was doing because she'd been grumbling since the new year that she wanted to try new things.

On Thursday 12 March, on the way home from work, Ben picked up a vindaloo for one. Makala didn't like spicy food, and besides, although he hadn't heard from her today, he assumed she would be going into town with the girls again. He was looking forward to a night in with a DVD and sole control of the remote. It was only when he couldn't find the movie he was looking for that he thought to call her. He tried her mobile but it was switched off, so he tried Devi's; no doubt they were together.

'Yes, yes, of course she's here with me,' said Devi enthusiastically.

Clearly they were holed up in a bar somewhere, probably Dylan's, Ben guessed as he heard the distinctive 'good time' sound blaring down the telephone line: clinking glasses, laughter, rowdy people shouting above other people's energetic conversations, and the latest will.i.am track pumping out behind it all. The house suddenly seemed very silent. It struck

Ben that it really had been quite some time since he and Makala had gone out together. They used to go out a lot; a new club, bar or restaurant wasn't considered open until he and Makala visited. But once they moved into their own place, it seemed such a waste of money to squeeze into noisy bars full of admittedly attractive but often drunk and arrogant types, all of whom had disposable incomes matched only by their disposable lifestyles. Such dens of iniquity and indulgence were unnecessary. All that pumping music and chat and expensive cocktails was only a means to an end. It was easier to get to it in the comfort of his bed.

Not that they did *that* much any more either.

'Can you put her on? I need to ask her where the *Fury* DVD is,' said Ben, pushing away thoughts of his paltry sex life.

'Oh, is that the one with Brad Pitt?' asked Devi.

'Yes.'

'And Logan Lerman?'

'Yes.'

'He's grown up hot, eh?'

'Erm, I don't really know. Can I speak to Makala now?'

'Now?' And then it struck Ben that Devi was not just making polite conversation; she was stalling. But why? 'Well, she's in the loo right now. I'll get her to call you when she comes out.'

'I could hold.'

'No, don't. My battery's almost flat. I'll get her to call you from her phone. You should check in the magazine rack for the DVD; sometimes Makala shoves things in there when she's tidying up. Bye.'

Ben listened to the dead line and then the silence of his home. There was a vast expanse of hush, metres of quiet, litres of the stuff, a perpetuity of nothingness, interrupted only by the tick-tock of the kitchen clock and the faint, mildly annoying buzz of something playing on a neighbour's stereo. He recognised the tune but couldn't quite place it. A little like Devi's tone. He recognised it but couldn't quite accept it. Devi was a reckless woman most of the time; fun-loving was the kindest thing people said about her when they were talking about her approach to relationships, but he'd always got on well enough with her. She was straightforward, up-for-it fun, but just then she hadn't sounded like herself. She'd sounded cautious. Hesitant. Not words you normally associated with Devi. Even above all that good-time noise Ben had heard that much. But why?

About five minutes later his mobile rang, Makala's caller ID flashed on the screen.

'Hi!' She sounded breathless. 'Devi said I missed your call. The DVD is on the table in the kitchen.'

'Why is it there?' asked Ben, irritated. 'We do have a shelf for DVDs.'

'You left it there. You lent it to Tom at Christmas and when he returned it he left it on the kitchen table, where it's stayed ever since. Anyway, I'd better get back to Devi.'

'Yes. Where are you, by the way?' He tried to sound casual. He felt it was critical.

'Where am I?'

'Yes.'

'We're somewhere new. A new place in town called the Ivories. Can you hear the piano?' Makala went silent for a moment and Ben could hear the melancholic notes of 'Blue River' drifting down the line.

'Sounds very nice.'

'Yes. It is nice. I'll see you later.'

'Makala?'

'Hmm?'

'You OK?'

'Yes. Why, don't I sound OK?'

'Yeah, you do. You just sound—'

'Can we talk about this later, love? I have to go. It's my turn to go to the bar. Bye.'

But something wasn't right. It wasn't the fact that Makala sounded exasperated that he was responsible for mislaying the DVD in the first place and yet had called and interrupted her girls' night out. Nor was it a problem that she was keen to keep the conversation short and get back to the bar – both those things were situation normal. It was something else. It was the piano. When he'd been on the phone to Devi, he'd heard all sorts of boisterous, boozy activity in the background; sounds that made him parched for a pint and a cheerful night out. But when Makala had called him back there was nothing other than the sophisticated, seductive sound of the piano tinkling in the background. No matter how much he trusted Makala, no matter how straightforward Devi generally was, there was only one conclusion to be drawn. He was being lied to.

Ben intended to sit down with Makala and ask her what the hell was going on. He was not the sort of man to tie himself up in knots imagining what might be going on. Another bloke would have leapt to the conclusion that his wife was having an affair, being unfaithful, treacherous. He might have sorted through her handbag or tried to get a look at her call log or emails to find evidence to back up his murky, mad meanderings. But not Ben; he was better than that. Makala was better than that. There would be some simple explanation for why she wasn't with Devi last night and yet had said she was.

He just couldn't think what that simple explanation might be.

Perhaps she was going for a new job and didn't want to discuss it until the position was in the bag. Although what sort of job interview took place somewhere that had a pianist, and why wouldn't she discuss it with him? They always talked about everything, especially the big things like job changes. Or at least they used to. It was true that Ben couldn't actually remember when he'd last asked Makala how her day at work had been, and although he knew she had a new boss, someone who'd started in January, he couldn't remember the bloke's name, let alone how well they were getting on. Maybe Makala wasn't happy at work, maybe she was interviewing for a new role, or . . .

Maybe Ben and Makala weren't talking as much as they used to.

But still, there had to be a less extreme reason for her lying about her whereabouts other than a sordid, filthy, sick little affair. Ben just couldn't see Makala pushed up against an alley wall, frilly pants dropped round her spiky heels.

Although they had once done exactly that. They used to have quite an adventurous sex life. They'd take any opportunity. In cars, outside . . . They were once staying at his parents' house and time on their own was at a premium, so they booked into a hotel for some afternoon delight; his mother assumed that his big grin at teatime was because she'd cooked him his favourite spag bol. But when did they last . . . ?

No, no, Makala wouldn't. Would she?

At that moment Makala walked through the door with her mobile still clasped to her ear. She was chatting and giggling until she saw Ben standing in the living room, then she said abruptly, 'Got to go. Talk to you after the weekend,' and rang off.

'Who was that?' asked Ben. He tried to make his voice come out calm and even. He did not want to betray the fact that he knew who she was talking to – she was talking to *someone*. Someone who'd kissed her lips, her body? Someone who had grabbed her ass? Someone who'd tasted her nipples? Pictures of

Makala writhing naked with an anonymous *someone* assaulted his brain. A scarlet pain split him open. He might vomit.

'A colleague,' she said.

Was this man she was screwing a colleague? Was he married too? The bastard. Did he have children? Makala was a bitch. Was it her boss? The boss Ben knew nothing about. The boss she'd been so secretive about.

'You're home early,' she said, keeping her eyes on her handbag, replacing her phone carefully in the side pocket. Since when was she so tidy? Ben wondered. Normally she dropped her bag on the floor, her coat on a chair, while her phone, car keys, post and half-eaten muesli bar would be scattered in a Hansel and Gretel trail from the front door to the kettle. Ben sank down into an armchair and wedged his hands under his thighs to stop himself doing any damage. He wanted to tear the house apart, tear their lives apart. No, no, she'd already done all of that. Adrenalin ricocheted around his body like a poison. Arsenic thoughts swelled through his veins. No, no, not this. He coughed to buy time.

'Yeah, I got to thinking, we haven't seen that much of each other recently. I thought it would be good to do something tonight,' he suggested. If she said yes, if she agreed to spend time with him, then he'd got it all wrong, he told himself. They'd be OK. They could have a chat and he'd get to the bottom of this. What did it mean, a few Thursdays out with friends; even a Thursday out not with her friends? What did it mean, a phone call, hiding her phone away? What did it all mean?

Nothing that Ben wanted to understand.

But everything would be OK if she just said yes. He looked at her beseechingly.

'That's nice.' She kissed him on the forehead. 'But I'm shattered. I don't think I can face another evening out. I'm going to have an early night.'

Noooooooooooo. Ben concentrated on breathing. In, out, in, out. Simple stuff, been doing it for years, but in his shock and terror he seemed to have lost the knowledge.

'Big one last night, was it?' he gasped. He could hear the sneer and suspicion in his own voice. 'Knackered, are you?' he snarled.

Shut up, Ben, you wanker, he instructed himself. What are you doing? What are you saying? This is *Makala*. She deserves your trust. She's your wife. Just ask. Ask straight out. Ask her why she lied. There will be a simple explanation.

'Hey, guess what? I'm going on a business trip next week,' said Makala. She sat down and eased off her shoes. She was wearing four-inch heels. Shiny, new, sexy shoes.

Just breathe. 'You are?'

'Yes. Isn't that great?'

His heart was sitting in his rectum somewhere. He could feel it, like lead. He really could. A physical pain that seemed to be dragging his body to the floor. He wanted to lie down. 'But you never go on business trips. You're an office administrator. You're needed in the office. That's the point,' he muttered.

'I know, but my new boss thinks I should have more responsibility,' she trilled.

'I'm sure he does.'

'It's some sort of conference for office administrators. In Nottingham, would you believe?'

No, he wouldn't.

'When?' Don't say Thursday. Not Thursday. Any other night but Thursday. Break the pattern. Show me there isn't a pattern, pleaded Ben in his head.

'Next Thursday, actually.'

So there was a simple explanation for her lying then, thought Ben. She was having an affair.

*

He watched her pack. She packed stockings.

'Why are you taking those?' He caught her secret smile before she replied; it took all his determination and self-control not to put his hand down her throat and wrench out her heart, eat it in front of her. That was what she was doing to him, after all.

'Oh, you never know when you need to dress up at these things,' she murmured.

As the door slammed behind her, Ben reached for the vodka bottle. He planned to drink more than he had ever drunk in his life. It was unbelievable to think he'd started drinking before breakfast TV finished; that wasn't acceptable by anyone's standards, but nothing was acceptable any more. He sent his boss an email saying he had a stomach pain and would work from home for the day. No one would question him. Ben was well liked and generally reliable. Even if anyone suspected he was lying, they'd turn a blind eye this once.

Ben realised that drinking vodka at nine in the morning was not big or clever, but he couldn't think what else he could do. He had always assumed he was the sort of man who wouldn't take any crap from a woman, especially not Makala. He'd watched a lot of films like *Rocky* and *Terminator* during his formative years; he knew the importance of being as hard as nails. He needed to strike quickly. Go on the offensive. Sever all emotional ties. A proper bloke (or alien) always won the day. That was what women wanted. He was and always had been a straightforward sort. He wouldn't expect Makala to put up with him being unfaithful and he wouldn't put up with her being unfaithful. He'd always said as much. Too much self- and mutual respect. That was what he'd said. But now that the distant and unreal threat of infidelity had spilt its bloody cruelty at his door, he wasn't so sure. Now, he thought he loved her too much to imagine a life without her. He couldn't see how Sylvester or Arnie could help. He was frozen. Petrified. Inert with disappointment and disillusion. He began to wonder, could he keep a lid on it? Maybe whatever she had going on with this other *someone* would blow over if he didn't draw attention to it. It might disappear. He'd always said he loved her too much to play second fiddle, to play games or to play away. Now he thought he loved her more than that.

There was no one to talk to. He had good mates, but they didn't talk about stuff like this. There was no need. He knew that if he told any of them that he thought Makala was shagging someone else, they'd call her a bitch and tell him to dump her. Job done. Discussion closed. 'Bitch. Dump her.' Three words. His life over.

But it wasn't as easy as all that. In the past week, since Ben had discovered that Makala was not out with Devi as he'd been led to believe, he'd found (to his dismay) that the fact that she had betrayed him did not make him hate her. The possibility that he might lose her made him love her more, not less. How could he explain that to his mates? It was an irrational, undignified response. But then, what was rational and dignified about love? He didn't know any more. His world had turned upside down.

Ben had started to notice things about Makala that he'd forgotten. She smelt delicious. She was really pretty, especially now that she was making an effort again. Oh God, the agony: she was making an effort for another man. When she applied her red lipstick this morning, was she thinking about this other someone kissing it away? Probably. The thought made him ill. He'd watched her so carefully this week; she was smiley, sexy, sweet. How had he stopped noticing?

He'd listened to her too. She chatted about stuff all the time; lots of it was the usual crap – which of her friends was seeing someone/buying a new sofa/getting a promotion – but when he'd listened carefully this week, he'd realised that even this trivia wasn't actually boring when Makala was talking about it. She had a funny way of relaying anecdotes and she was always so nice about everyone, it made for pleasant listening. Why had he stopped listening to her? How could he have taken her for granted? He hated the fact that someone else was hearing her stories now. And this someone else would be hearing the very best stories, the stories people told each other when they were first dating, the stories that made the teller look eternally amusing, resourceful and interesting. Oh God, he wanted to pull this man's ears off. Rip out Makala's tongue. Do anything, anything at all to stop them talking.

Talking.

If only it had stopped there. But it hadn't. This someone was clearly going to be spending the night with his wife. Was it the first time they would sleep together? Or just the first time in a bed? Ben banged his head against the sitting room wall, trying to dislodge the terrible images that had taken up residence in his brain.

This was no good; he couldn't just stay here and get drunk. He needed to do something. Anything. He decided to take a walk into town. He could buy a coffee, sober up a bit, try and formulate a rational plan.

It was cold, and relentless March drizzle soaked him through within minutes, but Ben didn't care. Even if it had been a bright sunny day he'd have hated it. He did not find the walk the respite he was hoping for. Every shop and café reminded him of Makala: places they'd visited together, eaten together, breathed together, just been normal and together. He thought he saw her on every street, imagined he spotted the back of her coat in every doorway. She had a new coat now. A blue one. She'd picked it herself, brought it home; she'd even wrapped it. He hadn't so much as transferred the money from his account to hers, and yet it was supposed to be his Christmas present to her. How could he have been so churlish, so careless? Why hadn't he come into town before Christmas and taken an hour to pick out something nice for her? Maybe a pair of earrings, or some boots; he knew she would have been chuffed with whatever he'd chosen.

Defeated, Ben bought a bottle of red wine and a six-pack of beer. He might as well go home again, get plastered as he'd originally intended. All his thoughts were glued to the past; he couldn't formulate a plan for the future. And then suddenly he did see her. Oh God.

It was true then. She was not at a conference in Nottingham. She was here in Birmingham. He'd kill her. He'd kill him. Whoever he was. The bastard. The fucking nasty bastard who had stolen her. And then he'd kill himself, the stupid arse who had let her go.

Makala adored hotels. Decent ones with discreet and polite doormen, ones with impressive, dramatic lobbies and rooms with dim lighting and plush furnishings. She loved the clunky wooden coat hangers that waited in the wardrobe, ready to take on the personality of the new guest. She was excited by the luxury of a mountain of cushions scattered on the bed; Ben hated the idea of cushions as decoration and they only had two tatty, overused ones in their entire house. She liked the neat, clean, sparse bathrooms and the fact that however much mess she made, she wouldn't be cleaning it up. She actually squealed with excitement when she opened the minibar and was faced with the diminutive bottles of spirits, wine and champagne. Once she had mastered the dinky CD player and selected an appropriate chill-out track, she opened the champagne. Why the heck not?

Makala thought that affairs were delightfully easy to slip into, especially when carried out in this amazing other-worldliness. It was almost a wonder that so few people went this way – what was the statistic she'd read back in late January when she came up with this plan of action? Thirty-three per cent of women and forty-five per cent of men, something like that.

Of course there were times when she felt guilty about what she was doing. She did wonder what she'd got herself into but she found that she couldn't stop, not now. It was too late, she was in too deep. She had not been lured into this situation by the dizzying thought of a new and other man. She had started this as a reaction to the deep grief she felt at the loss of the passion between her and Ben.

Ben. His very name bubbling up in her head made her heart thunder. In the beginning, she'd been so attracted to his voluble excitement, his manliness, his sexiness. He had been hilarious, droll, swift and confident. Even charming when he wanted to be, yes, charming. Her friends used to comment that he was besotted. Besotted, what a marvellous word that was. What a marvellous thing it had been. Where had all that disappeared to? Had it been smothered by conversations about the importance of house contents insurance and whether magnolia or a deep colour would work best on the wall in the downstairs loo? Not that they even talked about that sort of stuff now. Every room was freshly decorated. They appeared to be done.

They used to happily, irresponsibly spend a fortune on meals out at tiny bistros, evenings in funky bars and even, occasionally, weekends in hotels just like this one, in Bath or Edinburgh. It had all been so glittering. So dreamlike. So buoyant, unique, gleaming and exciting.

She pushed Ben aside. This was not the moment to think about him. It hurt too much. Saddened. Right now she was going to have fun. That was what this was all about, after all – her need, desire for fun. That was what she had wanted from her Thursday nights. And it was working. Her 'independent Thursdays', as she liked to refer to them, were giving her a new-found (or rather, a retrieved) sense of confidence. Doing new things with new people was exciting. She felt buoyant and unique again – to an extent. Not quite in the way she used to with Ben, in fact not anywhere near it, but she had at least found the will and the energy to start visiting the gym again. Being out and about rather than slumped in front of the flat screen had led directly to her regaining a sense of the importance of 'making the best of herself', as her mother called it; 'personal grooming' was how the glossy mags referred to her reignited vanity. It boiled down to the same thing. She'd had her roots done for the first time in months, and she'd been waxed in areas that she'd forgotten existed. She'd started to bother with body moisturiser, and she liked looking down at her hands and feet and seeing pretty manicured nails. She'd done them herself last night in front of the TV; it was good use of the dead time, although Ben had moaned about the smell of the varnish and said he thought it was unnecessary to paint her nails for a work confer-ence. Yes, he was right: for a work conference such preparations would be redundant. She'd said nothing.

And there was nothing to say now, either, as she pulled back the pristine bed sheets and climbed in.

Afterwards, when the sheets had been crumpled and their innocent, immaculate state consigned permanently to the past, and after a room service tray of goodies had been delivered and devoured and the tray once again dumped outside the door, Makala slipped out of bed and quietly drew a deep bath. As she dimmed the lights, swallowed the last dregs of champagne and stepped into the warm, cocooning water, she felt bubbles fizz inside her body and out.

Suddenly there was a banging at the door. What the hell was it? It was loud and persistent. She hadn't ordered any more room service. She waited a moment. More thumping. A fire? No, not a fire. A man's voice. No, it couldn't be. Ben.

Makala leapt out of the bath, not caring that water sloshed

over the brim and soaked the floor. She grabbed a towel and wrapped it round herself, not even taking time to pull on one of the hotel's fluffy robes.

The door inched open slowly, reluctantly. But to what end? What was the point of buying time? It wasn't as though her lover could go anywhere. Ben stared at his wife, shards of pure fury shooting from his eyes; he wanted to lodge his pain in her soul. She clung to a large white bath towel; her knuckles were grey with pressure but her face – her face, goddammit – had never looked more beautiful. She was flushed and pretty. She'd never looked more alluring, satisfied or tempting.

'Let me in! Let me in!' he yelled. She didn't have much choice. He was making so much noise that someone would probably call security soon. He didn't care. He pushed past her roughly.

The room was just as he'd imagined it: posh and hot. The sheets were tangled, and one of Makala's shoes was lying on the floor next to a champagne cork. He'd spent all evening imagining this scene of sleaze and sin. After spotting her in town at lunchtime, he'd followed her back to her office. He'd waited outside all afternoon, sheltering in a doorway over the road. She'd emerged dead on 5.30; keen, he'd thought bitterly. She was carrying her small overnight case. The code to the lock on the case was the date of their wedding anniversary; he wondered if she'd remember that when she opened it up. Maybe she would; after all, she'd remembered their anniversary this year although he hadn't.

She'd walked to the King's Hotel. He'd guessed that that would be where she'd go for her sordid little fumble, because she was always going on about how they should have a meal there one night. He lingered outside whilst she checked in, and when she headed to the lifts, he entered the lobby and made straight for the bar. It was very chic; there was a pianist. It took all of Ben's self-control not to seize the poker from next to the open wood fire and smash the piano into tiny pieces.

He'd waited and watched. It was difficult to identify exactly which man was her lover. It was a busy hotel; the lobby filled and emptied several times and Ben couldn't keep track of all the men who came and went. He drank whisky. Straight. Three of them, quite quickly; the barman started to offer him water and ice and he asked for a card to start a tab. He guessed he wasn't making an especially fine impression. He reasoned that he ought to stop drinking, it wouldn't help things – then he ordered another.

He waited until 10 p.m. They were the longest hours of his life. He had time to think about all the occasions he'd said he was too tired to go out with her, although he could usually find the energy to go for a pint with his mates; and he had an age to think about all the times he'd tuned out of what she was saying or interrupted her to tell his own news. He wondered when he'd last bought her flowers. He couldn't remember. He wished they'd spent their money on a holiday last year, instead of buying the TV. Maybe he should have done a bit more of the cooking or the ironing. She really hated ironing and he was quite good at it. He had lots of time to think it all over.

He didn't dare risk arriving at her room too early, before her lover got there. Who knew, perhaps this scummy man wasn't planning on making his booty call until later, maybe after he'd been home to see his own wife. On the other hand, perhaps they were already getting down to it and the man wouldn't spend the night, so as not to make his wife suspicious. It was hard to judge it. In the end the decision was made for him. He saw his chance when there was a changeover of staff on reception. He paid his bar bill, retrieved his card and then used it as proof that he was indeed Mr Hendy, husband to Mrs Hendy who had checked in earlier. It was a relief that Makala had used her own name. Ben supposed she'd have to, so she could pay with a credit card.

Irrationally, this thought annoyed him too. What sort of man had she hooked up with? Why wasn't he paying for the room? How could this bastard treat his wife so cheaply? The thought had sent new spears of fury through his body.

He had swallowed the bile and said as calmly as he could to the receptionist, 'No, don't ring up, she might be sleeping. I'll surprise her.'

'Where the fuck is he?' Ben demanded.

'Who?' she asked.

'Don't you dare! Don't you dare treat me as if I'm some sort of idiot. I've worked it all out. The Thursday nights out with the girls, ha! The renewed gym membership, ha! You're not at a bloody conference, are you? Where is he?'

'Who?' Makala demanded more forcefully now.

'The man you are in love with. The man you've started to make an effort for, wear heels and lipstick for.'

Ben was screaming now. His spittle hit Makala's forehead. She couldn't take her eyes off his Adam's apple. It was pulsing wildly. She'd always found his Adam's apple strangely sexy.

'He's in the bathroom,' she muttered.

'Hiding, is he? So he should. I'm going to bloody kill him.' Ben strode towards the bathroom and flung the door open. Empty. He checked behind the shower curtain. No one.

Makala carefully put her arms around her confused and furious husband. They watched their own reflections as she snaked her hands over his chest.

'I don't understand,' said Ben. 'Where's your man?'

'That's what I've been asking,' said Makala quietly. 'But now I see he's back.'

Ben was unable to comprehend, so carefully she explained. 'You're looking at my man. There is no man but you. Never was. Never will be. But you'd stopped seeing me. I had to do something drastic to get you to look my way again.'

'An affair?' Ben's eyes were misting up. She hoped he wasn't going to cry. She wouldn't mind for herself – in fact she'd quite like it – but he'd hate it.

'No, nothing that drastic. I just wanted you to think that maybe . . .' She shrugged.

'You're here alone?'

'Not now, baby. Not now.'

The Hen Night

'So, what are we doing exactly?' asked Zoe's mum, as she plopped on to the comfy squashy settee and reached for a sausage on a stick.

Jess had been unsure about how to cater. Champagne and smoked salmon canapés seemed too frivolous for the occasion, but egg sandwiches and sherry seemed too funeralesque. In the end she'd plumped for sparkling white wine and nibbles on sticks.

'It's an intervention,' said Jess, Zoe's best friend since infant school. 'It's an American concept. We all agree that Zoe should not be marrying Todd, don't we?' Zoe's friends and relatives exchanged glances (ranging from guilty to assured) and nods (ranging from apologetic to emphatic). 'Well, the purpose of tonight is to persuade her to ditch him. For her own good.'

'But she thinks you've arranged her hen night?' asked Chloe, Zoe's cousin.

'Yes.'

For a moment Jess's confidence and conviction wavered. She should have stopped Zoe buying a new outfit for tonight, the night on the tiles that was unlikely to materialise. At least not if Jess had her way. It was such a shame, she thought. Zoe really did look knockout in those new skin-tight jeans and the floaty black top, and she'd looked more and more fabulous over the last few weeks – probably because of the upcoming wedding. Jess was stabbed with feelings of guilt. How could she inflict so much pain on her best friend?

She breathed in and reminded herself that the creepy Todd had as good as assaulted her. His drunken pass had been so obvious and insistent. It wouldn't have been so bad if he'd been shamefaced or repentant the morning after, but instead he had winked at her over the cornflakes in Zoe's kitchen! Even so, Jess would probably have left well alone if the incident had been isolated. But when she'd mentioned it to Fran, the other bridesmaid, Fran said that he'd had a crack at her too. Then Jess whispered her misgivings to Chloe, and Chloe confided that none of the family liked Todd much either.

'He owes me money,' said Zoe's aunt. 'I paid for the wedding cake and the cars. I wouldn't mind, but he's always talking about how much he earns yet he never spends a penny of his own. He could peel an orange in his pocket.'

'He didn't notice that Zoe has lost nearly a stone for the wedding, and she's been working so hard at her diet and exercise,' said one of the cousins.

'He called her lardy the other day. Lardy and lazy. I heard him with my own ears or else I would have doubted it,' pointed out Fran, shaking her head in disbelief.

'He's the one that's idle,' added Zoe's mother. 'Zoe does everything for him. She even cuts the lawn at his flat.'

'And he knocks the booze back,' added Chloe.

'Nothing wrong with liking a drop,' said Zoe's dad. 'But he doesn't know when enough is enough.' It would be his sole contribution to the evening; no one expected him to offer much more. It was good of him to turn up. Interventions were newfangled; it was agreed that they were women's work. Zoe's dad was only here in case things turned ugly. He had a calming presence. His wife of forty-two years claimed he couldn't get into a lather in a bath full of Imperial Leather body wash.

'And he has shifty eyes,' concluded Mrs Davis. Zoe and her son had courted for two years when they were teenagers. She'd always hoped . . .

'OK, so we have our reasons,' said Jess, more to convince herself than anyone else. The crowd was baying for blood, but she knew it wasn't going to be easy. She understood how much Todd meant to Zoe and how much time and effort Zoe had put into planning the wedding. The wedding that was due to take place next week, with a string quartet, fireworks and six small flower girls. Oh lord. If the wedding was cancelled, Zoe's nieces would never forgive Jess.

Jess had long suspected that Todd was not the right man for Zoe. Zoe never seemed relaxed and happy in his company. More often than not they were fighting or Zoe was walking on tiptoes to avoid a quarrel. But they'd rubbed along for months, and months had turned into years, and then years had turned into an engagement. Todd didn't go down on one knee and produce a ring. Nothing as formal as that. Apparently one of Zoe's great-aunts had died and left Zoe a sapphire ring. Todd had joked that it would save him a bob or two if they ever did get hitched. After that Zoe had started to wear the ring on her third finger, left hand.

Where had confident, carefree Zoe vanished to? thought Jess. Who was this downtrodden woman left in her place?

Jess understood the need for companionship. She understood the embarrassment of attending friends' *second* weddings, let alone first weddings and children's christenings, without the chance of reciprocating. She wanted to meet the One, fall in love and get hitched too. She was old-fashioned enough to think it would be a nice thing to do – but not with just *anyone*, or worse, someone like Todd. It had to be the One. Zoe used to say the same thing. How could she be thinking of compromising?

The final straw had been when Todd started to go on about Zoe getting a boob job. Apparently he didn't like 'tiny itty-bitty titties'. That was probably why he'd felt entitled to grope Jess and Fran, who were both well-endowed. Jess had the sort of boobs that shuddered just a little when they escaped from her bra at night. Fran had proudly breastfed for the best part of a year. She claimed that when she heard a hungry baby cry, her breasts, unbidden, would jump into action, even if it wasn't her own child.

Zoe had been waiting for her breasts to grow since she was ten. Now, twenty years later, she accepted that it wasn't going to happen. Still, she saw it as a good thing that people never glanced at her chest when she was talking to them, at least never more than once. Todd had said he didn't know how a fat bird could be so flat-chested. He'd said Zoe was a freak of nature. He'd started to cut out articles and adverts about plastic surgery from the back of Sunday supplements. He'd said that instead of a honeymoon, perhaps he could go away with the lads for a few days and Zoe could get her boobs done.

Jess shuddered. It wasn't right. Why couldn't Zoe see that it wasn't right? She checked her watch. Zoe was due any minute. Never mind butterflies – Jess had kangaroos in her stomach. She needed the loo. She needed a drink. She needed the night to be over. Maybe she should keep her trap shut. They could drink the fizzy wine and then go to a club. This could be Zoe's hen night after all. No one wanted to hear that their man was a loser. What if Zoe didn't believe Jess? Or she believed her but still hated her for making it impossible to ignore Todd's lecherous ways? Many messengers had been shot for less.

The front door banged. This was it. Zoe strode into the small sitting room crammed with her friends and family. She was wearing her new jeans and looked as wonderful as Jess had expected.

'Oh, hello, Mum, Dad, Mrs Davis, I wasn't expecting you here.' Zoe wore an expression that Jess, her oldest friend, didn't recognise. She appeared triumphant, terrified, excited and depressed all at once.

'I invited them,' explained Jess.

Zoe looked surprised, then relieved. 'You are so *the* best friend,' she whispered. 'You knew, didn't you?' Jess tried to smile to hide her confusion. Knew what?

'Jess has done absolutely the right thing in gathering you all here,' Zoe declared. 'I don't know how she does it, but she's read my mind. I have something very important to announce. I'm sorry, but the wedding is off.'

Stunned silence. 'Did you find out he made a pass at Jess?' asked Chloe.

'No,' said Zoe, shooting Jess a quizzical look.

'You know he owes me money?' asked Aunt Lil.

'No.' Zoe looked sorry.

'You're sick of his moody, greedy, rude behaviour?' asked Fran.

'No,' said Zoe firmly. 'Well, maybe.'

Jess wanted to ask if it was because he'd been obsessed with the outer package and never considered Zoe's inner beauty. But she couldn't quite bring herself to talk boobs in front of Zoe's dad.

Zoe turned pink and shrugged. 'I've met someone else. Rik, you can come in now. It's as good a time as any. Come and meet my mum and dad.'

It's Got To Be Perfect

Jonah thought long and hard about the perfect place to propose to Lily. He wanted perfection as defined by big-budget Hollywood rom-coms; nothing less than endless ticker-tape celebrations and soft-focus moments. Lily, with her fabulous sense of humour, honesty and sexiness, deserved nothing less.

Jonah's father had not shared Jonah's view. He'd proposed to Jonah's mother over a bag of fish and chips as they'd huddled close and looked out at the grey English Channel. Apparently his father's line of reasoning was that if they got married, they could have sex somewhere more comfortable than the back of Jonah's granddad's van. If Jonah's mother thought the wording of the proposal left something to be desired, she must at least have admired his honesty. She'd replied, 'OK.'

Jonah would've paid cash not to be privy to this information, but his father loved to relay the story and diligently repeated it every wedding anniversary. 'Smelt of salt and vinegar when I kissed her,' he'd say with a laugh. There had been thirty-eight anniversaries so far.

Jonah and Lily had lived together for two years now and they could have (or not have) comfortable sex whenever they wanted. But this seemed to increase rather than diminish the expectation that the proposal had to be something splendid and exceptional.

Jonah bought a square-cut diamond solitaire, set on a platinum band. It was hideously expensive, but the jeweller told him to suck it up, and pointed out that now he was proposing, he could expect his credit card to be bashed on a regular basis because weddings, especially perfect ones, cost. The sobering thought dramatically altered Jonah's fantasy about where to propose. The beaches of Barbados, the Maldives and Thailand were all dismissed, as was Venice (smelly), the top of the Eiffel Tower (crowded) and Rome (frantic). He didn't want to do it in a restaurant – or anywhere public, come to that. It had to be somewhere personal, unpredictable and, well, perfect.

After lengthy agonising, he decided to book a cottage in Wales for a weekend break.

'Wales?' questioned his brother.

'Yes.'

'Remote cottage, is it?'

'Yes.'

'So she can't run away?'

'Do you think she might?' Jonah was suddenly terrified.

'You're punching above your weight with Lily, mate. But hell, why not? Go for it.'

The drive took five hours in Friday traffic, but it was worth it. They arrived as the sun was setting behind the rugged gothic hills, creating a mauve-and-peach evening sky punctuated by strong, imposing smudges of scarlet. The clouds looked like those a child would paint with a thick brush. It was breathtaking. Jonah nearly spluttered out the proposal on the spot but didn't; he needed to chill the champagne, find his iPod (he'd uploaded a careful selection of romantic ballads) and put the flowers he'd brought with him in a vase. It all had to be just right.

The cottage was split into two sets of accommodation, which

Jonah hadn't realised when he'd made the booking on the web. He was a bit disappointed and anxious; he hoped the other half would remain unoccupied, as the last thing he wanted was forced intimacy with other holidaymakers. For the next forty-eight hours he wanted Lily all to himself. He unpacked hastily and slammed the champers in the fridge, but he couldn't find his iPod and he only had time to pop the flowers in the sink before Lily called him into the bedroom.

After they'd made love, Lily decided she wanted to explore. Ideal, thought Jonah, he'd ask her as they mooched to the pub, cocooned in the warm evening air. But as he searched around for a place to conceal the engagement ring (maybe he should've packed baggier trousers; why hadn't he thought of that?), he became aware that Lily was talking to someone.

'Of all the places!' said a male voice, before bursting into a hearty laugh. Lily squealed with excitement. Jonah rushed outside in time to witness his girlfriend enveloping a bloke in a warm hug. A hot embrace, some might say.

'Jonah, this is Daniel Carter,' said Lily, beaming.

Daniel reached for Jonah's hand and shook it firmly. Mutely, weakly, Jonah allowed his limp wrist to be shaken about. Daniel Carter: the name slowed his blood. Dan the Man. *The* ex in the flesh – toned, tall, tanned flesh at that. Jonah noted Dan's big blue eyes, broad shoulders and bulging biceps. Really, Lily had undersold him when she'd once commented (casually, as though she didn't think it mattered) that he was possibly the most beautiful guy on the planet. If it stopped with good looks, Jonah might have been able to smile and chat, but he knew that Dan had completed an Ironman triathlon, and that he was a human rights lawyer. He probably had Obama's personal email as well.

'What a coincidence. I thought this place was pretty much deserted,' said Dan, with a broad, relaxed grin that exposed perfect white teeth lined in a neat row.

'It's a bit secluded,' agreed Lily, nodding.

'Intimate,' chipped in Jonah defensively.

'You must have dinner with us,' offered Lily.

'Dan probably has plans,' mumbled Jonah.

'No, not really. That would be wonderful, if you've enough to go round. I haven't packed anything. I thought there'd be a corner shop,' smiled Dan, as though he was completely unaware that he was ruining Jonah's life.

Jonah had planned delicious menus for the weekend and bought the produce accordingly; normally Lily did the lion's share of the cooking and he'd wanted to indulge her. He'd spent hours in the local deli, elbow to elbow with passionate foodies and fraught, determined housewives who wanted to impress their dinner guests by buying local and organic. He'd bought the best of everything: fresh pasta, ripe cheeses, crusty bread, black olives slathered in virgin olive oil, caviar and smoked salmon. Lily went inside the cottage, opened the fridge and assessed the contents. The men followed. Dan's step was jaunty, Jonah's demoralised.

'Oh, we've loads. It'll be nice to have someone to share all these gorgeous goodies with.' She reached for the pasta, olives and smoked salmon. Jonah bit his lip and didn't point out that the salmon was intended for breakfast; he'd been planning on making Eggs Royale.

The evening was the worst of Jonah's life. Instead of proposing to the woman of his dreams, he was forced to watch as she zealously flirted with her ex lover. Dan was undeniably interesting, engaging and charming. Under different circumstances his anecdotes might've even made Jonah smile, but tonight Jonah wanted to gouge his eyes out with the cheese knife. Was it really necessary for Dan to be so well informed about *every* subject broached? No, Jonah thought not. And even though Dan ostensibly tempered his galling good looks with a sprinkling of self-deprecating stories, Jonah wasn't fooled. He knew the man was an arrogant, seducing, champagne-guzzling jerk. He could absolutely tell by the way Lily laughed at everything he said.

Yes, champagne-guzzling! After they'd consumed the two fine bottles of wine that Jonah had bought, Dan spotted the champagne and suggested opening it. He promised he'd replace it tomorrow, but that was unlikely: there weren't any shops nearby. Besides, Jonah didn't want to toast his engagement with champers bought by his fiancée's ex.

Assuming there was to be an engagement.

The more Jonah drank, the more he doubted there would be. He became increasingly morose as he watched sparks fly between Dan and Lily, sizzling and cracking in the air. As he downed more Merlot than he knew was sensible, he asked himself why these two had ever split up in the first place. Had she ever said? Maybe, but it was a long time since they'd had that sort of conversation. Why things hadn't worked out with an ex was something discussed in the first month of a new relationship or not at all. Jonah couldn't remember why Dan and Lily hadn't made it, and judging by Lily's animated manner right now, she couldn't recall either. She clearly thought the man was perfect. Eventually Jonah stumbled upstairs. He'd leave them to it. It was less painful.

The next morning Lily crawled out of bed and returned with two large tumblers of water. Their hangovers were so severe that sex was out of the question, but her bringing water was a comfort, not just because his mouth was as dry as a sand pit, but because the act was considerate and domestic. Maybe he was getting things out of proportion, being a bit paranoid. The birds were singing, the sun was slicing through the gap in the curtains – it was a good sign. He would stick to his original plan: they'd go for a walk, eat a picnic and he'd propose on the Brecon Beacons, where the lush green hills would roll out in front of them like possibilities.

He moved the dead flowers out of the sink – he hadn't taken the time to look for a vase; he'd forgotten all about it when Dan arrived on the scene – and did his best to cobble together a picnic, fighting his irritation that the wholemeal crusty bread had been eaten and they'd have to make do with basic white sliced, *and* that after he'd gone to bed, Lily and Dan had helped themselves to the organic lemonade, no doubt in a effort to abate the onset of hangovers, and gorged on the chocolate fudge cake, probably to quell the munchies. He took a deep breath. It was far from ideal – not what anyone would call perfect – but at least he'd have Lily to himself all day.

When Lily entered the kitchen, she was bleary-eyed and pale from last night's excesses, yet still beautiful. She'd paired up a flirty floral summer dress with big wellington boots. It was a good look for her: she had gorgeous skinny knees and smooth thighs, and the outfit somehow suggested vulnerability and femininity combined with a practical resourcefulness.

'Will you throw in another sandwich?' she said. 'Dan told me last night that he's just been through a nasty break-up. They were meant to be coming here together. I felt so sorry for him, I said he could tag along today.'

Jonah took a deep breath. So the demigod was single too; that was all he needed. 'You should put on a pair of jeans. It might turn cold,' he muttered darkly.

Dan offered to carry the picnic hamper; no doubt he'd hitch it up on one shoulder as though it weighed nothing. Jonah couldn't allow that – it was a matter of pride. Clinging martyr-like to the wicker basket, he trailed behind, forced to watch as the pair of them laughed and joked, as Lily touched Dan's arm, as they tilted their heads close to one another. Jonah thought he might be sick, and it wasn't the hangover. Normally he was not the sort of man to wrap himself up in angry knots of bleak imaginings. Jealous judgements and cruel conclusions ruined people's lives. That said, it was clear that this picnic would not present the perfect opportunity to propose.

'You've been really quiet today,' said Lily as she linked her arm into his on the walk back to the cottage later that afternoon. 'Everything OK?'

'Great,' replied Jonah, in a tone that suggested he was announcing the violent death of his favourite aunt.

'Is your hay fever kicking in?' she probed.

'No.'

Lily looked bemused. Dan was a few feet behind them, locking a gate they'd passed through, mindful of the country code. 'You just don't seem happy and I can't think why.' She gestured to the endless fields covered in merry buttercups. 'I mean, this place is wonderful, and Dan being here, well, it's *perfect*. It's been so long since I saw him and—'

'You know, I think my hay fever *is* kicking in a bit. I'm going to give the pub a miss tonight,' cut in Jonah.

'Oh, right. Well, as you like.'

Jonah watched from the window as Lily and Dan set off on the two-mile walk to the local. It was a gorgeous evening: the setting sun spilt pink light on the country road, a cat circled Dan's legs; it was disgustingly idyllic. He pushed his hand deep into his trouser pocket and felt the ring box nestled forlornly there. Did jewellers do returns? he wondered. It didn't matter; getting the money back on the ring wouldn't help.

He planned to drive straight back to London first thing tomorrow. Dan could drive Lily. He'd get out of the way; retire with what was left of his dignity.

Or he could hide in Dan's place until they returned, catch them at it and cause a big, ugly but ultimately satisfying scene.

He plumped for the latter. Dan's door was unlocked. Jonah mooched about, unsure what he was looking for. It felt bleak. Dan hadn't unpacked anything other than his washbag, and there really wasn't any food (Jonah had doubted this). The only personal touch was a framed photo of him and some other guy, his brother presumably, which sat on the bedside table.

Suddenly Jonah heard Lily's voice through the open window. 'Thanks for coming back, Dan. I couldn't enjoy myself in the pub knowing Jonah's ill and alone.'

Jonah swore to himself and looked around for somewhere to hide. He hurriedly scrambled into the wardrobe. He listened to Lily's footsteps as she ran up the stairs in their cottage and then came outside again.

'He's not there.'

'Must've gone for a walk to clear his head,' suggested Dan. 'Look, while we're here, I'll grab that photo of Joe to show you.'

Jonah didn't dare breathe as he heard them climb the stairs and come into Dan's bedroom. Their footsteps tapped the wooden floorboards, making it easy to track their movements. Lily sat on the bed.

'Joe's a looker,' she commented. 'But Dan, you deserve more. You caught him having sex with your personal trainer. End of. You need a man of integrity, like Jonah.'

At that moment two things happened. One, Jonah remembered why Lily and Dan had split up and why she'd never felt any animosity towards or longing for her ex; and two, the wardrobe door swung open and he fell out on to the floor by their feet.

'Looks like I'm not the only one coming out of the closet,' laughed Dan.

'What are you doing in Dan's wardrobe?' demanded Lily.

Jonah wondered whether he could pretend to be looking for antihistamines to ease his hay fever, but the words 'man of integrity' stopped him. Instead he muttered, 'Would you believe I'm planning the perfect surprise proposal?'

'I see.'

'Marry me?'

'OK,' said Lily.

And when they kissed (after Jonah got up off the floor), he noticed she smelt of salt and vinegar crisps, a detail he planned to tell his kids.

A Blast From The Past

'I'm bored,' I groan down the phone to Anu.

'Of work. Of Ethan? Of life?' asks my best friend.

'The lot,' I grumble. 'It's all the same.'

'Sorry, zero sympathy. I'm nothing but envious that you've been happily married for two years. Try hauling your cookies on a new blind date every Friday only to have your already extremely low expectations dashed as you meet men who look like Quasimodo and have Homer Simpson's IQ. Or speed dating. Or try taking the Tinder swipe.' Her voice rises, hinting at how desperate she sees her situation to be.

I know, I know. In my head and heart I know that I'm far better off in a stable, happy relationship that might occasionally tip towards the humdrum, rather than still putting it about waiting for Mr Right and only finding Mr Just-About-All-Right. I know it in my head and heart – it's just a little bit south of my stomach that I sometimes feel restless. Ethan *is* my Mr Right. He can be clever, funny, thoughtful and sexy when he turns his mind to it. It's just we've been together long enough for him to believe he doesn't *need* to be any of these things on a regular basis. Seriously, I'm beginning to believe in the seven-year itch. I'm slowly turning my mind towards who is going to scratch it.

'It's just because we work together as well as live together that I get a bit fed up. There's no variety, no challenge,' I comment.

A tiny bit of me is wistful for those weekends on the pull that Anu still experiences. There's nothing quite like that feeling of expectancy and excitement as you push open the door of a trendy bar and are hit by the smell of aftershave and booze and the noise of confident, irresponsible chatter. I remember the slight thrill of stumbling across gangs of mysterious men in dark suits. Men who have just been paid and, for that night at least, are all about flashing the cash as they force their way through the crowds towards the bar and ultimately into some woman's psyche and bed.

Places like that are quite an aphrodisiac even if you are half a couple. Before Ethan and I got engaged and started saving for the wedding and then the house, we used to go to those overpriced joints two or three nights a week. Then we'd come home and rip each other's clothes off. I think it was the loud music, pumping into our brains and then rushing through our bodies. I'd always want to dance, even when there was no space. I'd fight a powerful need to whoosh and swirl, carving out my own private dance floor, which wouldn't have been the appropriate thing to do in those deeply stylish bars – not at all cool. I understand stripping. Music does equate to sex. It pounds and devours and replenishes and ultimately relieves. I prefer to make love to music, rather than in silence. It helps create the mood; whichever mood I want. Swift and frenzied or leisurely and seductive. To be honest, I'd have it any old way at the moment. Ethan and I don't go out much at the weekends now. One or other of us always cries off with 'I'm too knackered.' Not literally, you understand – if only. Knackered with work, and commuting, and bosses, and stresses, sadly.

'Jane, you're pathetic,' Anu says affectionately. Her no-nonsense approach has been earned after nearly fifteen years of friendship. Her frankness and fondness go hand in hand.

'Maybe.'

'Look, you know you're mad about each other. It can't be constantly hearts and roses; that is such an unrealistic expectation.'

I'm not after hearts and roses; I'm keener on stockings and massage oil. That's the sparkle that's been doused with familiarity.

'How's business anyway?' she asks in a blatant attempt to change the subject. I know she thinks I'm being self-indulgent.

'Fine, you know. It's just hard to get overly excited about selling car insurance.'

'You do OK on commission and you never used to complain. You said working in a predominantly male environment was hot,' points out Anu with a reasonableness that has a real chance of bordering on the annoying.

'Well, it was until Ethan and I clicked, shagged and married.' Getting married was the nail in the coffin as far as my harmless office flirtations were concerned. Suddenly I disappeared. 'Now there are no sneaky sparks darting over the water cooler whilst loafing with colleagues.'

I cast my mind back and trawl through a number of flirtations and dirty, fast liaisons. Working in an environment dominated by men readily supplied that much. I shiver with delight at the memories. I admit I miss the ego boost.

'My heart bleeds. I don't get the same opportunities in the beauty spa. Any men I come across are as gay as a maypole and just want me to wax their back, balls and crack so they can impress some chunk of hunk.'

I giggle at the thought. 'Does it impress, having hairless balls?'

'Don't know; it's a mystery to me. Men are. Straight or gay. It's desperate. I suppose it must have the desired effect, else they wouldn't keep coming back; I mean, the pain must be off the scale. Anyway, aren't you going to some sort of conference soon?' she asks. 'That will be a bit different, a change in routine at least.'

'Yup, in Blackpool, next week. Three days and two nights. I'm thinking of shaking off Ethan and snogging someone inappropriate,' I say flippantly.

I don't really mean it but I want to shock Anu. Or maybe a tiny, tiny part of me does mean it and admitting as much shocks *me*.

'A more sensible approach would be to talk to him about how you feel,' she says.

'I don't do sensible.'

'No, you don't, do you? How could I have forgotten that?'

It's the usual corporate dinner thing: big, indecorous and reckless. Everyone is really going for it, and now that I've given Ethan the slip, I can too. Drunken, not-too-fussy men stand in hungry gangs trying to impress women by shouting loudly and shoving one another around. Why they think that might impress us is beyond me; sometimes I think we are still in the school playground and that's where we'll always stay. Flushed, these guys reel about, their words and thoughts becoming hazy. The women are sweaty and surprisingly keen, as they've been enjoying way more than the odd glass of wine on the company expense account too. Tomorrow will be all about embarrassed, reluctant glances and hideous hangovers but no one cares about that right now. I find my table and name card, sit down and pull my face into a professional, polite smile.

It's him. It takes me some seconds to place him. As soon as I acknowledge him in my mind, I acknowledge him in my knickers too. A delicate, woozy sensation, at once tingling, exciting and unnerving. I met him years ago. Sometimes it seems like another lifetime. I wasn't expecting to see him here tonight. I hadn't expected to see him ever again, let alone find him sitting at my table. It's been such a long time. He gives me a slow, wide grin and it hits me between the legs. His eyes strip me naked. I can almost feel my slinky top drop to the floor. His eyes are sparkling green with golden flecks running through them. Suddenly I'm thinking sunshine dripping through the leaves of a dense forest and me running through said forest – naked of course. All domestic thoughts scamper to the dark recesses of my mind. I have no intention of airing them tonight. He has fine, transparent skin and high cheekbones. He is reasonably buff but not so it's intimidating. I'd say he's well defined, athletic but not bulky. He's been working out. He looks at me and his eyes level me. It's as though he knows all about me; all my secret, horny, unfaithful intentions. A nuclear explosion of emotion and instincts sparkles and splinters inside me, lodging in my head and my breasts. My knickers and heart sing as one. I'm quivering.

The familiar masses around us amalgamate into one indistinct and unimportant smudge and we're left alone in our togetherness. Together in our aloneness. I *have* felt lonely recently; I hadn't realised as much until I find myself languishing under his familiar but forgotten gaze. Lonely is a terrible thing to feel when you are married. I decide in an instant that I'm going to have him. Stunned and messed up by undeniable lust, I can't ignore the attraction between us. I can almost smell it. I'm sure I'd be able to taste it. I have to stop myself licking the air between us, for fear he'd think I am insane.

'I didn't expect this.'

'Nor did I, but take your pleasure where you find it.'

I don't know how he knows about my recent thoughts of discontent but he does. He must sense it and he's going to take advantage.

'So, Titch, want a drink?' He is already pouring me a glass of red (my preferred choice); that and using my nickname creates a tangible intimacy. Something I've been lacking at home recently. I search around my head for *his* nickname. I do vaguely remember he had one. What was it? It was something to do with his huge member, I recall that much. Donkey? Studley? I've got it! Stuffin.

As in Stud Muffin. Or I suppose the other sort of stuffing. God, we used to laugh at that. Calling out 'Ethan' during orgasm (fake or real) is so pedestrian in comparison.

We flirt to an unprecedented level. Within minutes I fall back into the flip and frivolous ways that were second nature before I married but have seemed redundant and superfluous of late. I suddenly feel like I am up there with every great seducer in history. I am as mysterious as Cleopatra, who bathed her sails in spices so that even from a distance over the seas her scent attracted her warrior, Antony. I am as irresistible as a dark and doe-eyed heroine from a black-and-white movie – he does want to come up and see my etchings; frankly, he just wants to come up. I am Mrs Robinson and my graduate wants me to roll my stockings off. To hell with the consequences.

I am straightforward and direct about my intentions and yet I'm slippery and vague when he tries to rush to pin down the deal. Our starters haven't even been devoured; I've no intention of giving it up yet, although he's already hinted that we'd catch up better in the privacy of one of the conference hotel's bedrooms. I manage to be direct and yet coy, a good bet but not a sure bet.

He is full of challenges and inconsistencies but they don't infuriate or frustrate me. Rather, he has the safe familiarity of an ex-shag but the tremulous expectancy of something approaching a new and unexpected level. He pours me another drink.

He talks about his job, which is the same as mine, therefore deadly tedious, yet somehow he manages to appear dazzling. He has funny customer-related stories to tell and I'm in peals. Ethan and I do the same job and we are more or less at the same level. Actually, I got a promotion on my grade last year, which he didn't, so technically I'm more senior. He said he was really pleased for me but I noticed that after that we stopped talking about work. It can get a bit tricky. Besides, what's the point, since we both do the same thing day in, day out? Cold-calling, following up leads, upgrading existing insurance deals; it's not like either of us works for the UN. But tonight I see that Stuffin can talk about our dull job in an amusing, interesting way. I wish Ethan and I could have these conversations over the dinner table.

Stuffin makes quite a wedge on commission because he has the gift of the gab and he's undoubtedly a charmer on the phone. He certainly is in the flesh; that much is true. I'd forgotten just how charming.

'Not that it matters how much I make because my wife spends it as fast as I can earn it,' he comments. I bristle and cough into my wine. I'm uncomfortable with his grumble about his wife. I don't want to hear it – not tonight.

I need to change the subject. Sex comes to mind. His too, apparently.

We talk about sex and remember the things we have in common, and discover some new things too. He confesses that he fantasises about three-in-a-bed scenarios, although he's quick to point out that he's only interested in two women and one guy.

'Sexist pig,' I comment. Then, more seriously, 'You're kidding, right?'

'Four tits, choice of goals, an abundance of flesh. It's every man's dream, isn't it?' I think I must look a bit concerned because he breaks into a grin and then reassures me, 'It's a fantasy. Relax. Truthfully, I'd probably never have the guts to go through with it, even if—'

'The missus said it was OK?' I finish his sentence.

'Exactly, even if she gave me her blessing, I'd no doubt bottle. I'm sort of old-fashioned in that one particular way. I like the woman I'm with to know that she's my focus.'

It's a pretty bizarre comment under the circumstances. I blush and reach for my wine. He stretches and gets there before me. His hand closes over mine and I swear I feel fireworks going off.

'I've just had a Brazilian,' I blurt.

'No way.'

'Way.'

'Why?'

'For a change. To be, I don't know, tidy.' I thought that area needed a little attention, a little TLC, though I can't bring myself to confess as much.

'Did it hurt?' he asks.

'A pain like no other, baby,' I laugh.

He laughs too, then picks up his wine glass and takes a gulp. 'I'll make it worth your while, sweetheart,' he mutters.

I screech indecorously and then push away my plate. Really, I haven't got an appetite, at least not for food. The evening zooms by in a flash of bright images and vibrant, overpowering smells. Expensive colognes shield perspiring bodies; the smell of poached Scottish salmon and tartar sauce becomes indistinct from the taste of metallic mass-catering trays. I can't decide what I can taste, what I can smell and what I can touch, see, hear. Stuffin is all. His presence overpowers every one of my senses and I can't or won't steady myself. The crowds around me are tremendously loud; laughter and exhilaration bang up against random lust and all-round expectation. Packing a suitcase has mysteriously led to a loss of propriety and sense of self for many other people. It seems everyone in view has abandoned social norms.

We continue on our exploration of sexual fantasies. I tell myself we're only talking; what harm can it do if I tell him what's really on my mind? Ethan and I normally talk about stuff like changing our electricity supplier or whether we should retile the bathroom. With Stuffin I am able to be quite a different woman.

'I'd really like to do it al fresco,' I giggle into my champagne (bought by Stuffin – a frivolous, expensive indulgence and twice as tasty because of that).

'I'm sure that can be arranged,' he says with a cheeky wink.

I gasp and pretend to be outraged. I mean, I ought to be outraged. I'm a married woman. Married women don't behave like this, I tell myself. But I'm not convinced. The fizz of excitement that is scuttling through my body suggests that, married or not, this is exactly the way I ought to be behaving. I feel more alive and magnificent than I have for months and months.

'I'd like to do it at my mum's,' says Stuffin.

'What?' Now I *am* taken aback.

'It would just be so naughty to slip out between the roast lamb and the apple pie and have dirty, fast, against-the-wall sex in her cloakroom.'

'That's actually quite weird.' I laugh somewhat hesitantly.

'It would be so risky. The idea of banging you against the wall and all her little bowls of smelly soaps jumping off the shelves is just too exciting. The fish and mermaid ornaments would be scandalised.'

This time I laugh out loud because that proves it: boys never grow up. I'm enjoying the thought that sex can be fun again. Recently whenever I've thought about making love to Ethan, I've counted it along with chores such as putting on another load of washing or tidying my sock drawer – something I really ought to get round to. I take another swig of champagne; it punches the back of my throat. The fresh, addictive dryness of a million bubbles dancing excitedly on my gums makes me confess, 'I'd like to be tied up.'

'Then I could cover you in cream . . .'

'No, champagne.'

'. . . and lick you clean.' We both fall silent for a nanosecond, then Stuffin says, 'I'd like to join the mile-high club.'

I add, 'I'd like to have sex in every room in my house.'

'I'd like to see you in very scanty panties, suspender belt, stockings, the works.'

'Can't manage that tonight, I'm afraid,' I tell him. I glance at the table and then look up at him from under my lashes. 'You see, I'm not wearing any underwear at all.'

He grabs my arm, nearly pulling it out of the socket, and dashes from the dining room.

'In there,' he says, pointing to the room that the conference delegates are meant to retire to for coffee after we've finished dinner. I noticed that as we left the dining room the sorbet dessert was being served. People will be filtering through in no time. It's very risky; maybe we should go to my bedroom. Stuffin seems to be reading my mind.

'In there,' he repeats. Clearly the risk factor is an attraction to him.

There are coffee cups lined up in neat rows, two huge urns of boiling water and plates of chocolate mints. But I know it isn't caffeine that's on Stuffin's mind. Barely pausing to check for privacy, he slams me against the wall and kisses me urgently. It's frantic, and hurried, and amazing. He grabs both my hands and pins them above my head as he pushes his body into mine and kisses me hard. He barely has to restrain me; I'm rooted. His kisses are strong, dark and engulfing. It feels as though I've never been kissed before. Or if I have, they were poor dry-runs. I feel his cock stiff and large against my stomach. He kisses me in all the usual places: my breasts, my neck and shoulders, head and hair. But he kisses me in unusual places too: my eyelids, my eyelashes, my nose. I kiss him back, and lick and suck and consume. He inches my skirt up, and his cool hand dances across my flesh. By the time he slips his fingers inside me, I am drenched by my own excitement. Ice-cold fingers on red-hot flesh: I come immediately, spurting out on to his hand. The exquisite release sends shocks plunging through my spine. With one hand he teases me; with his other he scrabbles with his flies and then almost instantly sinks into me. I stare into his glinting eyes and he stares back, never losing me. Not for a second. It feels astounding. It feels imperative. It feels right.

He's soaring, he's filling, he's plugging. He completes me.

It's over in minutes. But at this exact moment I know it will never be over.

'Again,' I mutter, breathlessly.

He nods. 'Not here. Outside.' He puts his cock away and I grab a paper napkin and rub away the stickiness of his love. I smooth down my skirt but all my attempts at grooming are wasted as I'm sure there is a big neon sign over my head announcing, *I've just been stuffed by Stuffin*. My lipstick is smudged into slutty streaks across my mouth and chin; my hair is scrambled where before it was neat and sleek. I pray we don't get spotted.

'Come on.' Again he leads the way, and I love it that he takes charge. At best I'd describe Ethan as compliant. He allows me to take the lead in everything, whether that's booking mini breaks or initiating anything in the bedroom; at worst I'd describe him as lazy and apathetic. None of the above is attractive. Stuffin grabs my hand and dashes me through the reception, seemingly oblivious to the curious looks we attract. His determination and confidence are an undeniable and irresistible turn-on.

'Over there.'

He points towards the pebbled beach. It's pitch black now. I hope the cloak of night-time will protect my modesty, because I get the distinct feeling Stuffin isn't giving that much thought. He's clearly hungry to tick off my al fresco fantasy and, giddy and exhilarated, all I want is more.

My throat is dry and tight and my hands are clammy. I feel nervous and delighted all at once. We fling ourselves to the pebbles and immediately start pulling at each other's clothes, swiftly, expertly undressing one another. He tugs my spangled top over my head and flings it to one side. I don't even care that it's not machine washable and that that extravagant display is going to cost me a trip to the dry cleaner's. I'm naked from the waist up and my skirt is bunched to my hips. He takes off his jacket and shirt and is wearing his trousers on one leg. I treat myself and allow my eyes to fall slowly from his face down to his broad shoulders, down to his ever so slightly rounded stomach, down to his evident passion, past, and down to his legs, which are strong and hairy. I lie facing him. After an unhurried viewing, I return my eyes to his face and find that he is staring at me as though he's never seen me before. With bold delight I wait as his eyes fall from my lips to my breasts to my mound. Suddenly he lunges and kisses me there. Slowly, so slowly he kisses and licks and nibbles, until I whimper with pleasure. I lie back carefully; my flesh – naked and exposed – is occasionally jabbed by a rough pebble. No doubt my back and buttocks are going to be black and blue tomorrow, but I hardly notice the discomfort, let alone care about it, I'm so involved with what he's doing to me. Stuffin *is* concerned and wiggles me on to our now damp and crumpled clothes.

I can smell the sea and feel invigorated and high on it. Bit by bit, little by little, his tongue explores my body; he kisses me and rediscovers zones of delight that make me wail and burble simultaneously: my ear lobe, the ends of my fingers and toes, the crook of my elbow, the back of my knees. He gently bites my stomach and sucks my tummy button. When I think I can't take any more and I'll explode with wanting if he persists in his gentle exploration, he suddenly plunges. He dives, he shoves, he scalds, seizes and pulls until I cry out with a violent mix of pain and desire.

I am worn out with rapture, but I can't let it all be one-way. I don't want to appear lazy. He's already come once tonight and I'm not certain of his recovery rate, but I have to give him the opportunity. I push him on to his back and kneel over him. He makes me feel so sexy, an undeniable expert. He groans, writhes and slithers beneath me. I grab hold of his cock, tugging up and down swiftly and expertly until he quivers and becomes breathless. Finally he yells out, a terrifying holler that must have alerted the more conventional lovers – those who are walking along the pier – to our secret whereabouts.

'Shush,' I giggle as I scramble to pull on my top just in case anyone comes to root us out.

He pulls me to him and says, 'Just hold me a while.'

My hair is damp with exertion and is glued to my neck. My tits are wet with his kisses and my stomach and thighs with his love. We hold each other close until our breathing relaxes and we inhale and exhale in unison. His hands smell of sperm; I do too. But I feel clear and cleansed. He cups my face in his hands and we stare at one another. His face radiates an elated, confident ruddiness. He seems so deliriously certain of everything. I hope I'm mirroring him. I imagine I am.

'I am the luckiest man on the planet, do you know that, Titch?'

'You can call me Jane again now,' I say with a contented sigh.

'I love you, Jane. You are the perfect woman. How many other wives would have the guts to admit that things were becoming a bit predictable and instigate this whole "let's pretend we've just met" thing?' He shakes his head with genuine respect.

'Not many, Ethan, not many.' I smile to myself. 'All the fun of a real affair—'

'Without any of the messy bits.'

We can hear voices, probably teenage boys, and they seem to be getting closer. No doubt they are looking for somewhere to swig their cans and smoke, but I don't want to be part of their teenage education. We scramble to our feet and dress quickly.

'My top will have to go to the dry cleaner's. Can you drop it in, and I'll pick it up? You'll probably have to take your jacket too,' I tell him.

He laughs. 'Red alert, wild abandon disappearing,' he teases.

'Well, at least until you take me on holiday. We still haven't ticked off joining the mile-high club,' I point out.

'True. In that case, I'll pop in to the travel agent when I drop your top off at the dry cleaner's,' he says as he leans in for a long, slow kiss that hits me south of my stomach.

Grating Expectations

It wasn't entirely Maya's fault that she had such specific expectations about the trip to Venice. Everyone agreed that a proposal was more than likely. Everyone being her mum, her sister and her four closest friends (one married, two single, one gay: a reasonable cross section of society – at least Maya's society). After all, Leon and Maya had been living together for four years – admittedly in *his* flat with *his* name on the mortgage and utility bills, but Maya bought the groceries, she'd redecorated the place from top to bottom, and her clothes were squashed into the wardrobes and bottom drawers; that meant something.

They travelled club class. Which was an unnecessary luxury for a short-haul flight and therefore, Maya thought, proof positive that Leon wanted this to be a particularly special weekend. Her preference was that he'd ask her fairly quickly, right at the beginning of the mini break. Perhaps tonight? Then they could utilise the rest of the time planning the wedding, or, rather more accurately, Maya could spend the time telling Leon what she wanted for her big day. She had very clear views on the subject. She'd selected the church, venue, menu, band and bridesmaids. She had a good idea about the style of dress she liked, though all the wedding magazines agreed you didn't really know until you actually tried it on which one would be perfect, so finalising that detail would have to wait.

Leon wasn't into big romantic gestures, so there was a reasonable chance he'd mess it up and propose somewhere unsuitable, like on the plane or in a restaurant. Maya had never liked the idea of restaurant proposals. A few of her friends' boyfriends had gone down that route and the girls always claimed to be happy enough with it, but Maya knew she'd be put off her food and she didn't like waste. Besides, how did you hug and kiss with a table in between and everyone watching? Maya talked non-stop on the plane so that Leon wouldn't find an opportunity to ask. She chattered about the bread rolls, her ankles swelling on flights, whether it was worth sending postcards, anything rather than him ruin her big moment by proposing somewhere inappropriate.

They emerged from the airport and Maya was thrilled to see a beautiful mahogany boat waiting to take them to the mainland. As they slipped through the water, the sun shone down and made everything appear glittery, the breeze lifted Maya's hair and she felt like a Bond girl. Now the boat limousine would have been an *ideal* place to propose, she thought.

'Isn't this just perfect?' she said, staring intently at Leon.

'Bit blowy,' he replied, without taking his eyes off the map he was scouring.

Leon had an innate distrust of foreign taxi drivers and always insisted on making a big deal of following their chosen route from airport to hotel on a map so as to ensure the cabbie took the most direct path. Secretly Maya doubted that he had any idea how to read a map of the sea and waterways, but felt it would be rude to point as much out.

It was about four o'clock by the time they dropped off their bags at the hotel. Leon suggested they went straight out to make the most of the late-afternoon sunshine, perhaps buy an ice cream. Maya agreed but insisted on taking a quick shower and changing her outfit. She didn't want to be proposed to wearing the jeans she'd travelled in. In the end it took about an hour and a half for her to shower, exfoliate, reapply make-up and select the outfit she did want to be wearing when she agreed to become Mrs Johnson. Unfortunately, by that time the sun had slipped behind a large cloud. Leon grumbled and commented that stilettos were impractical footwear for foraging around the cobbled streets of Venice.

Maya was in love with Venice. She'd known she would be; she'd decided it was the most romantic place in the world the moment Leon mentioned he'd booked a mini break. She'd read all about the Doge's Palace; for weeks now she'd imagined them strolling through Piazza San Marco and taking a trip to the Accademia.

Venice did not stink; Maya had never believed it would, despite all the grim warnings she'd had from people like the woman in the nail salon, Dan from next door and the lads in the post room at her office – people who didn't have an ounce of romance in their bodies.

They mooched around the baroque back streets, stood outside churches and wandered across umpteen pretty bridges. Despite the lines of washing flapping in the breeze, Maya thought these streets had a shabby charm and were a perfect backdrop for Leon to pop the big question. Clearly he did not agree; he kept resolutely silent despite her numerous hints about how *romantic* everything was, and how *perfect*. They ambled along the waters of St Leon's Basin. How was it described in the guidebook? A mirror to reflect the majesty and splendour of the Basilica of San Giorgio Maggiore. True enough. A perfect place for a proposal. Maya dawdled. She leaned her elbows on the iron railing of a bridge and gazed out on to the canals as though enchanted. It was a lovely view, although she hadn't expected to be in the shade of the buildings quite so much and wished she'd worn long sleeves. In her imaginings they were always walking in the sunshine. Leon leaned his bum against the railings and looked in the opposite direction; Maya tried not to be disconcerted.

'Leon, isn't this just so wonderful?' Maya gently bit her lower lip. Last week they'd been watching *The Graham Norton Show* on TV. They'd ordered a takeaway and opened a bottle of wine. They'd chomped their way through half a box of Milk Tray – not the type of confectionery Maya would ever take to a friend's dinner party, but in fact their favourite. Graham had been interviewing Hollywood's latest hot actress, who kept biting her lower lip. Leon had been mesmerised.

'Do you have a mouth ulcer, love?' he asked.

'No, why?'

'You keep chewing your lip. I thought you were in pain. I've got some Bonjela in my washbag. I'll dig it out for you when we get back to the hotel.'

'I don't have a mouth ulcer.'

'Maybe you've started to bite your lip as compensation for not biting your nails.'

She'd always been a nail biter; Leon hated the habit and had often urged her to stop. She'd tried on countless occasions but had never gone longer than two days without caving in and having a nibble; that was until she imagined something sparkly on her third finger left hand. Chewed nails would so ruin the effect.

'No,' she mumbled, somewhat exasperated. Clearly her provocative lower lip biting was doing nothing for Leon. She looked around for something to talk about, but despite the wealth of history, culture and bars, she was stumped. They endured a fifteen-minute silence, the first of their relationship.

Eventually Leon asked, 'Do you fancy something to eat? The local squid pasta is supposed to be worth trying.'

'I'm tired, let's just go to bed,' and so that he was absolutely clear, she added, 'To sleep.'

Saturday followed the same pattern. Maya woke up hopefully and dressed in a way that she thought appropriate for accepting a proposal. Leon woke up bewildered and a little bit resentful that a romantic mini break in Venice hadn't culminated in even a whiff of sex. Despite the top-notch hotel with four-poster bed and everything. His bewilderment and resentment grew as Maya spent the day acting increasingly weirdly. Normally so relaxed and such a laugh, she'd started to behave in a way that defied belief. Did she think he was a complete moron? He wasn't impervious to the dawdling at Kodak moments and outside jewellery windows. He knew what she wanted, she was being obvious, but frankly her behaviour was terrifying.

He *had* been going to do it. Of course he had. Why not? The girl was a marvel, he adored her. Or at least he thought he adored her. But her peculiar, pushy behaviour was making him . . . nervous. Suddenly he didn't like the way she munched her food, and her walk was funny, sort of lopsided. This wouldn't have been a deal breaker under normal circumstances, but what was normal about your girlfriend holding a gun to your head full of emotional bullets that she so clearly wanted to spend?

He'd planned to take her to Santa Maria Gloriosa dei Frari, arguably one of Venice's most sublime religious treasure troves, to see Titian's gloriously uplifting *Assumption* altar painting. He'd wanted to propose to her in front of that painting; he too was capable of assuming, planning and plotting. But her needy expectations had ruined everything. He felt she was presuming, second guessing and, worst of all, waiting. Now he thought he might return to England with the princess-cut diamond still in his jacket pocket.

By Sunday they were barely speaking. Maya insisted that she didn't want to go to a market (unheard of); Leon said he had no appetite for visiting restaurants (a first). Instead of enjoying the café orchestras, cooing pigeons and constant traffic of waiters serving alfresco diners, Maya complained that St Mark's Square was too boisterous. She rushed towards a gondola, no longer envisaging romantic opportunities (she'd given up on that; they were leaving early the next day) but wanting desperately to be away from the crowds, which as far as she could ascertain were made up entirely of besotted lovers.

They drifted gently on a gondola, moving away from the tourists. Maya stared at the stars glistening in the navy sky and wondered if she could be bothered to comment to Leon that the scene was perfect. He'd only ask, 'Perfect for what?' in an impatient voice, as he had done every other time she'd helpfully pointed out the ideal moments on their trip. Not that there had been so many today. Of course everything was still as interesting, steeped in history, culturally amazing as when they'd first arrived – only somehow not so perfect now.

Leon asked the gondolier to stop singing. He whispered to Maya that he had a headache, although she'd never known him to suffer from them before. He also muttered that the whole experience had been excruciating and a rip-off at fifty quid per person for twenty minutes' entertainment. Maya wondered what to do next. She supposed she'd have to finish it. Their relationship was clearly going nowhere fast. She couldn't just sit around and wait for Leon to finally decide she was the girl for him – or worse, perhaps decide she wasn't. Her ovaries were shrivelling by the minute; she didn't have unlimited time.

But she loved him so.

She couldn't imagine life without him. It was all so depressing and wrong. Nothing was turning out as she'd hoped, and now she could even detect unsavoury wafts of something pungent from the sewer, and stale sweat from the gondolier's T-shirt.

Leon felt miserable. Really low. He'd thought the break would be such a laugh. He'd splashed out: good flights, cool hotel, reservations at the best restaurants – not that they'd actually honoured a booking as yet. He wondered if the jeweller accepted returns. What a waste. Things couldn't get any worse, unless of course he lost the ring.

Panic! He frisked himself in a frantic attempt to track down the little box.

'What is it?' asked Maya.

'The ring! I've lost it. On top of you being a freak, I've lost the damned ring.'

'What?'

'Sorry, I didn't mean to call you a freak.'

'That's OK. I meant the other bit. What ring?'

'The engagement ring, of course. Christ, it's dark. Can you see a ring? It cost a fortune. I can't believe this! It's a blue box. Will you—'

'Yes. I will.'

'Look for it!'

'Oh, right. I thought you meant—'

'I'm unlikely to propose at the moment I've lost the ring, am I?' snapped Leon.

Maya was already on her hands and knees. She'd forgotten that she was wearing high heels and a white skirt. She groped around the damp gondola floor. Her bottom bobbed up and down and something shifted back into place for Leon. Maya no longer seemed overly keen or controlling. She was concerned and well-meaning again. His gut turned.

'I'll do you a deal. If you find the ring, I will propose, OK?' he laughed.

'Deal. And if I like the ring, I'll accept,' she added with a grin.

Something Old, Something New, Something Borrowed, Something Blue

The door bangs, the house trembles, I hold my breath. Bridezilla is home. It was my son that coined the phrase, and though normally I try to minimise teasing between my children (a lifetime's habit, a lifetime's work), frankly I couldn't agree with him more. She lets out a terrifying scream, which causes me to drop the potato peeler, wipe my damp hands on my skirt and dash to the hall, where I find her literally pulling at her hair and stamping her feet. She kicks an enormous box towards me. It's almost comical, except she's my baby – my twenty-seven-year-old baby, but my baby still. I fold her into my arms.

'Hush. Harriet, don't. Stop it, please.' I ease her tight fists from her hair and at the same time start walking her towards the sitting room making soothing noises.

'The dress! My dress!' She's livid; every freckle on her face seems to be tight with tension and fury. I'm almost afraid of her. Where has my contented, comical, serene daughter gone, and why have I been left with this despot?

When Harriet first called me to say that Jason, her boyfriend of four years, had proposed, I was delighted, ecstatic. Everyone was. They're a great couple, very loving and compatible, and besides, a wedding! Who doesn't love a wedding? So many of my friends have given up on the idea of their children ever getting married and have started to accept the word 'partner' (even though our generation can't help but associate it with business, or worse still, cowboy movies!). My friends say things like 'Well, he's like a son-in-law in every way, and who needs the expense of a wedding?' I've said the same myself, not daring to admit that I think weddings are beautiful and that I'd gladly plough our savings into that joyous day, given half a chance. I believe that marriage is hopeful, wonderful. OK, not every day, I admit. Quite a lot of the time it's about dirty socks, dreary admin and pretending to be entertained by stories that have long since become familiar!

However, secretly and on some low level, I've looked forward to Harriet's wedding from the moment she was born. Not that I was obsessed with the Big Day. I wasn't the sort of mum to talk about it when she had a first date ('Might he be the One?!') or when she went to her prom ('That dress, but in white – perfect!') or when she had a party to celebrate her twenty-first birthday ('At your wedding we'll do favours but get the same woman to do the flowers!'). Lots of mothers do regularly have this sort of conversation with their daughters, but not Harriet and me. That said, over the years, I had occasionally indulged in the daydream. I imagined a day oozing with laughter and champagne, surrounded by friends and family, Harriet centre stage, radiant, relaxed.

It hasn't been quite like that. The relaxed bit, well, that's been notably lacking.

I had to adjust my vision almost immediately when she dismissively referred to the ring Jason had presented her with as 'the holding ring'. She said she liked the antique emerald but it wasn't exactly what she had imagined; apparently she'd always wanted three round brilliant-cut diamonds, exceptionally white, with very few inclusions, held in a classic claw setting. Her precision took me aback. Who knew she'd ever given it that much thought? Apparently she had very clear (and expensive!) ideas about *every* aspect of the wedding. The Saturday after Jason proposed, Harriet cleared out a shelf at WHSmith, gathering up countless wedding magazines, her 'arsenal' she said with a determined grin; I've come to see them as the instruments of my torture.

Wedding planning is a black hole. A girl can get lost, Alice in Wonderland style, chasing down that dirty, deep warren of choices and information as she relentlessly strives for perfection. Things have changed since 1982, when Mick and I said 'I do'. We were happy serving jacket potatoes and chilli con carne; we had a cash bar. No one complained, no one stayed sober. We were considered flash as we had colour-coordinated balloons tied to the back of the chairs. Not helium-filled ones, mind; just the ordinary ones. Every time someone moved a chair, a balloon would get caught and explode. *Bang, bang, bang.* It was like a showdown at the High Chaparral. How we laughed.

Harriet hired a calligrapher to hand-write the hundred invitations. Each was tied with a silk ribbon, the envelopes stuffed with lavender. At the reception, the day after tomorrow, the chairs will be covered in white silk with huge pink bows; there are to be ribbons around the stems of the glasses, too. The favours are hand-made Belgian chocolates. They cost about the same as I spent on my dress, and I'm factoring in inflation. There are to be four bridesmaids, four flower girls and six groomsmen; doves and a choir at the church, fireworks and a live band at the reception. As if the day itself wasn't big enough, she's had endless rehearsals: hair, make-up and vows.

Mick and I had put a bit by. Harriet was extremely grateful for our 'contribution', but she and Jason had a savings plan to cover the majority of it. I mean, I can't complain that she's bleeding us dry, but Mick muttered about it for days. He's old-fashioned and proud; he thought he'd saved enough to pay for everything. I did too, really. We'd amassed a reasonable amount. But there's nothing reasonable about this wedding. Jason's parents also contributed; even so, Harriet has burned through the money. The dress was a particular bone of contention. She picked out a designer one at a fabulous London store; it cost over £4,000. I can't pretend it wasn't beautiful; it was shimmering, intricate, breathtaking. But £4,000! Even she balked at that. Compromises had to be made. In the end she decided to buy a copy online from China: total cost, including shipping, £190. I warned against this route; couldn't she simply find a less expensive dress? I suggested.

Hysterical Harriet lies on the couch as I tentatively pull the dress from the box. I see. Rather than the blush pink she ordered, the dress is practically scarlet. It is not elegant silk chiffon but polyester, and the beading is plastic rather than Swarovski crystals. Frankly, undeniably, it looks like a fancy-dress costume. It's a horror. 'Look, we can fix it,' I say, although I can't think how. 'We can buy something new.'

'The wedding is the day after tomorrow, Mum!' she yells, spraying angry spittle.

'There are off-the-peg designs. You're a standard size.'

'I'm fated!' she wails in despair. I have to admit that she's had a run of bad luck. Her best friend, the chief bridesmaid, broke her leg on the hen weekend. She's struggling, hobbling around on crutches. Harriet was not what anyone would describe as sympathetic. 'She'll ruin the photos!' she moaned.

'Have a heart, love. She's in lots of pain.'

'She was go-karting under the influence. I have no sympathy!'

Then last week the flower girls, all four of them, came down with chickenpox. They are past the infectious stage, but again, it's not exactly a good look on the photos. The vintage car Harriet had hired finally gave up the ghost, and so instead of the midnight-blue Rolls, she's having to manage with . . . oh, I forget what, something white anyway. And to top it all, the florist called yesterday to say that calla lilies have been blighted this year and might Harriet consider roses?

Harriet must have been mentally running through the tally of problems too, because she turns to me, wet-eyed, anger dissipated and vulnerability shining through. 'This wedding is fated, Mum, isn't it?'

'You've never been the superstitious type,' I remind her.

She holds my gaze. 'Do you think someone's trying to tell me something? Maybe we're not supposed to get married.' The thought forces a fat tear to roll down her cheek. I squeeze her hand.

I switch on the TV in an effort to distract her, then, ignoring her request for something stronger, go and make a cup of tea. I'm no sooner in the kitchen than I hear a blood-curdling scream, the sort she gave when she fell out of the apple tree aged seven and was concussed. Almost dropping the mugs, I dash back into the sitting room.

'Look, look, it's gone up in flames.' Harriet is pointing to the TV, where the local news is reporting a dramatic fire in a beautiful stately home. It takes me a moment to realise that the National Trust building in question is Harriet's reception venue.

'Oh my goodness, that's terrible. It's such a beautiful building. Are they managing to get it under control?' I think of all the ancient paintings and treasures housed there; they've endured for centuries, some of them. It's a tragedy.

'What am I going to do?' yells Harriet, not giving any of the important artefacts or antiques a thought.

'Well, we have insurance.' For all the effort put into sourcing a bubble machine, favours, Mr & Mrs ceramic coasters and edible gold glitter, it appears the insurance is the only really useful thing.

'That's it. I'm calling it off,' she shouts.

'What?'

'You heard, I'm cancelling.'

'A postponement might really inconvenience a lot of people, darling. What about Jason's family? They're flying in from the States, and—'

'Not postponing. Cancelling. This wedding has been beset with disasters. They're omens. Jason and I aren't supposed to get married. If we can't do it right, then we shouldn't be doing it at all.'

With that she flounces out of the room and upstairs to her old bedroom. It's like being in a time warp, transported back to her teenage years.

She's wrong, of course. Panicked. As she was wrong when she told me she would never pass her exams, never get a boyfriend, always have acne. I think back through all the traumas and tantrums that sit between us, part of the delicious, indescribable and indestructible bond of mother and daughter. I love her so much, and no matter what she's just said, I know she loves Jason too.

I take a deep breath. My eyes settle on the offending cardboard box. The dress is ugly, I can't pretend otherwise. Suddenly I feel a huge wave of sentimentality for my own wedding dress, which is stored upstairs in the attic, alongside my mother's 1950s wedding dress and one or two other items of treasured clothing, old photo albums, letters and books. Things I can't find room for downstairs but that flutter in and out of my consciousness and are forever treasured. I believe having a peek at those things might be quite comforting right now.

Carefully I climb the ladder into the attic; dust on my knees, I push my way through the cobwebs and boxes. I know exactly which one of those boxes cradles my wedding dress. I reach for it, open it, then pull the dress out to hold it against me. I have to stoop to avoid the beams and I'm aware I'm being watched.

'I hope you aren't going to suggest I wear that,' Harriet mutters sulkily. I turn and grin; her head is poking up through the floor. I beckon her to join me.

'No, the moths have got to it.'

'Oh, I'm sorry.' Harriet seems crestfallen. It's been a while since she's had any empathy for anyone else.

I grin and shrug. 'It doesn't matter, it's only a dress. Your dad and I are still going strong.' She looks uncomfortable. I'm not sure if it's because I'm making her think of me and her dad, or because I'm making her think.

She pulls herself up into the attic. Contrary to expectations, the dusty, warm wood emits a smell that is somehow comfy and inviting.

'What's this?' She picks up an envelope, tissue-thin paper, spidery handwriting.

'Besides people, that is the one thing I'd hate to lose in a fire. The one thing I consider irreplaceable. My mother gave me it on the eve of my wedding; I was planning on giving it to you on the eve of yours. Go on, read it.'

As she reads, I watch her lips move. I know every word.

Dearest love,

You must not be so panicked. So depressed. Now that men are coming home injured, or worse still, not coming home at all, I understand that you are fearful for me, but don't be. Be steady. Chin up. You are right, the nights are long and the dawn is shattered by the clamour and turmoil of explosions and the now-familiar long screech of the shells rushing through the air. Do you know how I drown out the roar of fire as the artillery erupts with enormous violence? I think of our wedding. The soft calmness that it will be. Don't worry that you won't have a new dress. Of course I understand that such things are hard to come by. You look adorable in that blue cotton dress you were wearing when you waved me off. Why don't you wear that? I like your idea of

picking flowers from the woods; it's been so long since I've seen
flowers. I can almost taste the ham pie and pickles you're planning.
I agree we don't need a tiered wedding cake. How clever you are
to think of saving jam jars to make night lights. It's good of Mrs
Ashworth to lend you her bunting; that will look ever so pretty
hung in the garden. It's going to be perfect. We're going to be
together. There's going to be a future for us.

Write soon, my love.

Yours for ever,

John

'Did he make it home?' Harriet turns to me with tears in her
eyes. The softness has returned to her face; she still looks
desperate, but now I know it's desperation for a happy ending.
I dig about and find what I'm looking for; I hand her the photo.

'That's your great-grandmother's wedding. And that's John.'
The groom is sitting in a wheelchair. 'He lost his foot, but you
know it never really held him back. They were so happy, from
all accounts.'

Harriet's eyes scan the photo, soaking up every detail.
'Everything is as he described. The bunting. The jam-jar lights,
the food on the table.'

'Yes.' It's a black-and-white photo, but I somehow know she's
wearing a blue dress.

'Everyone looks so happy.'

'Don't they?' I pause, a beat. 'I think I have some bunting,' I
say. 'We can hang lights in the trees in our garden.'

'It's the perfect wedding,' she murmurs, then laughs. 'But no
ham pie. Maybe fig and goat's cheese quiche instead.'

Adele Shares . . .

My Holiday Treats

Holidays are all about indulgence, treats and a break from the norm. My holiday starts the day before I go away with a mani and a pedi. I sort of love and hate the experience at once because I have very ticklish feet, so the bit with the filing thingy – that's torture – but a holiday would not be a holiday if I had scruffy nails. More often than not, I pick crazy colours, a vivid blue, a shocking pink or a sunshine yellow. I also like to buy some new books. I often take five or six books on holiday with me. After I've read them I give them to people I meet around the poolside or simply leave them in my hotel room or apartment. Spreading the love of a good book is part of the treat, but my actions are not entirely altruistic because I then have an excuse to go shopping – I mean there is no point in going home with a half empty suitcase, is there? I usually buy something for the house that reminds me of the trip, offering me comfort when I clap eyes on it in the bleak mid-winter. I've bought a beautiful carved wooden tray home from San Francisco, some stunning stag coat hooks from Canada, a gorgeous painting of Gaudi's Sagrada Familia from Barcelona and edgy alphabet prints from Amsterdam.

I'm a firm believer that the most precious thing in life is time.

It's such an obvious concept but we're all often so busy we forget that simple truth. Money comes and goes, time just goes so ipso facto time has to be more valuable. Therefore, for me, the biggest holiday treat is taking the time to enjoy the things that make me happy. Below I've listed a few of them. Some are big, some smaller but added together I think of them as my smile list. It's worth noting this is not the finite list of life's treats.

The feeling of sun on my skin; a bowl of fat, tasty strawberries; a cold glass of champagne; going out for the first time in a new outfit; the smell of steaming syrupy, black coffee brewing; a massage; taking photos; laughing so hard it hurts; the first cup of tea of the day; dancing until you sweat or ache; fresh flowers; bubble baths; putting the last piece in a jigsaw; fairy lights; being healthy; not acting my age but acting my shoe size; kissing; sunsets; sunrises. My Family.

What's on your smile list? Let me know!
@adeleparks #LoveIsAJourney

Fancy taking a trip?

Here's a taster of some fabulous locations that feature in Adele's novels!

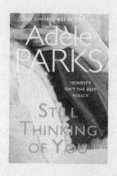

Join Tash and Rich who want to make their wedding vows on the top of a mountain in the Alps. What could be more perfect or simple? But never forget that love is complicated and happy endings can so easily melt away in **Still Thinking Of You.**

'Oh my God. Oh my God,' said Tash, as she jumped up and down on the giant bed. Rich started to put their passports and travellers cheques into the safe as Tash dashed around the suite.

'Have you seen in here?' she yelled from the bathroom. 'There's a hot tub.' Rich smiled at Tash's excitement.

'I guess I've gotten a little spoilt with travelling with work. I've forgotten the excitement of searching through the complimentary soap basket.'

This was exactly what Tash was doing at that moment.

'That's just what Jayne said about airports. How can you become accustomed to such splendour?' she asked, wide-eyed and incredulous.

'Ah, Jayne, yes,' Rich called through to the bathroom. 'There's something I need to tell you about Jayne.' He should have told her straight away, as soon as Jayne's name came up. It was just a bit of history, no big deal. He would have mentioned it already only none of the others had a clue either. It was awkward.

Tash bounced (because she'd lost the ability to walk calmly) towards the window and pulled back the blinds to admire the view. 'Wow!' they chorused.

The snow was falling quite heavily now. Avoriaz was perched on the top of a sheer cliff that plunged more than a thousand feet into a narrow valley below. It was a ski town quite unlike any other in France. The view, a fascinating mix of eerie and spectacular, was breathtaking. The hotel had large windows from which you caught the view of the Alpine setting of all the Portes du Soleil ski areas.

'Can you see how the form of the buildings echoes the sheer faces of brown slate that they sit on?' asked Tash. 'When we were driving in I noticed that, from a distance, the staggered heights of the multi-storey structures, the hotels and apartments, blend perfectly into the topography. They must have designed this place with quite some thought.'

Rich stood behind Tash, wrapping his arms around her body and resting his chin on the top of her head. He squeezed her tightly; she made him so proud. It was true, the resort buildings were unobtrusive. He'd noticed that, but he hadn't made the connection between their design and the topography of the mountains. Now that Tash had mentioned it, it was obvious. He loved the things she noticed, the things she said, the way she thought about things. It would surprise Mia, but Rich considered Tash the brightest woman he'd ever met.

'I read about the architect of this hotel. His name's Jacques Labro. And des Dromonts was the very first building constructed in this style, the style that became the distinct Avoriaz style,' added Tash. 'That was, like, half a century ago. Isn't it cool to think that this hotel set the architectural pace for the entire resort?'

They both fell into a comfortable silence again and watched the snow fall. They were both thinking about the fact that every child learns: no two snowflakes are alike. They were both thinking that this wasn't a surprise. After all, no two people are alike. Neither felt a need to say anything.

After a while Rich said, 'You know, it's possible to ski to Switzerland from here.'

'We should,' smiled Tash.

And that was another amazing thing about Tash, her 'can do' attitude. He loved that adventurous spirit in her. He was sure if he came home from work one day and suggested selling up and moving to Africa or Japan or somewhere, she'd simply say, 'What should I pack?'

'Thank you for bringing me to such a stunning place,' sighed Tash. 'It's beautiful.'

'Thank you for agreeing to come and . . .' Rich turned Tash around so she was facing him, 'and most importantly thank you for agreeing to be my wife. You've made me happier than I'd ever imagined it was possible to be.'

The couple giggled, almost embarrassed at how easily they had fallen into using clichés to describe their love for one another. It was odd to them that they used words other lovers had used because they were sure no one had ever felt as happy as they did now. They started to kiss and all memory of either Jayne or the rendezvous time was forgotten.

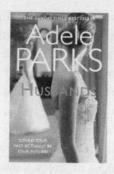

They say 'What happens in Vegas, stays in Vegas', but Laura is not the sort of girl to go on holiday with a married man. How will she feel when she finds out that's exactly what Stevie is? Things can only get worse when she finds out who he is married to. Love is complicated in Husbands.

Vegas is hysterical.

It's bloody hot without the luxury of air con, even so we reject the monorail and decide to walk along the Strip. We start, as is tradition, at the famous neon sign that states 'Welcome to Fabulous Las Vegas, Nevada' – risking life and limb running in front of cars to secure our photo opportunity – then we cross back to the west side of the street and start to walk north. Instantly we are thrust into one of Vegas's busiest junctions, where Tropicana Avenue crosses the Strip and connects casino hotels on all four corners. Thousands of pedestrians ride up and down elevators and escalators or rush and stride across the elevated walkways. Stevie and I stare at one another slightly fazed and momentarily purposeless.

'Look at that, we're in New York.' I point to a hotel fashioned as the New York skyline.

'That's so Vegas, baby,' laughs Stevie. 'You can see the Statue of Liberty, Brooklyn Bridge, even the Empire State Building and you don't have to leave Nevada. You've always wanted to see the Empire State Building, haven't you?'

'I still do. I'm not going to be fobbed off,' I joke even though I'm secretly pleased that Stevie has remembered my ambition. We spend a few moments admiring the Chrysler Building, Times Square and the Manhattan Express and then wander on. It quickly becomes apparent that Vegas is a city that's all about more. That which could be said is shouted, that which could be sung is belted out. Las Vegas, even on a hot afternoon, is a twinkling, flashing and glittering extravaganza. The city soars and scrambles, up, out and across, while neon signs of every shape and size imaginable jostle for attention.

The fantastical playground is a source of constant surprise. Stevie and I are amused by just about everything we see; it would in fact be impossible to take any of it seriously and still be certifiably sane. Only in Vegas can you see the Arc de Triomphe, Montgolfier's balloon, the Eiffel Tower, the Colosseum and an Egyptian pyramid without having to walk further than twenty metres. Only in Vegas can you watch a perfect dawn and splendid sunset, every hour, indoors, while doing your shopping, or stand by the kerb as a volcano erupts every fifteen minutes, or watch a sea battle between scantily clad sirens and nasty-looking pirates.

During this show a super-fit guy starts chatting to me about the weather (a bit of a non-starter, I thought, as we are in the desert and the weather is basically hot, day in, day out). I hold tightly to my bag, wondering if he's going to grab it and dash off. It's not until Stevie stares him down, and the guy merges back into the throng, that I understand. 'Was he coming on to me?' I ask. Stevie nods and grins. I blush, embarrassed. 'Did I lead him on?' I had chatted in an animated way, it's natural, I'm excited. 'Did I come across as flirty?'

Stevie laughs. 'It's not your fault! The man has eyes, and you're gorgeous. He was bound to try his luck.'

I'm gorgeous. The thought makes me giddy but, even so, I

spend the rest of the day avoiding eye contact with tasty men and worrying about VPL. I have not thought about Visible Panty Line for years. But, if I'm the sort of woman men chat up in the street, I might be the sort whose arse they look at too. No one wants to be objectified but I find it difficult to be indignant. Stevie's attention and affection are creating a halo of attractiveness around me and I like it. I like being desired.

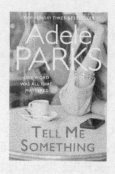

Go with Elizabeth and Roberto to visit stunning Verona. They are looking for their new beginning in Tell Me Something.

Verona is as beautiful as I could have hoped. It's full of Roman remains, rose-red medieval buildings and romantic dreams of young love. I arrive bouncing with hope and excitement, as Roberto and I have chatted non-stop for the entire journey. I've amused him with stories about our customers and I've had the opportunity to fill him in on the details of my new job. He seems interested and is very encouraging. He's told me a little bit more about his plans for the bar. He wants to landscape the outside area (currently used as a dump for our old furniture, worn tyres and similar junk). He wants an impressive outdoor eating space that will attract families during the daytime and rowdy parties at night. We discuss the menu changes that we might introduce for the summer and Roberto agrees with me that the old-fashioned loos have to be replaced with modern, clean and stylish ones. I have not asked him exactly how he spends his siestas or how he and Ana-Maria split up and made up. I don't want to spoil the atmosphere.

Roberto knows Verona well and quickly finds street parking that is within easy walking distance of the main piazza. Piazza Bra is a large, open space dominated by the Roman amphitheatre.

The piazza is rammed with tourists, who are chatting, taking photos and tripping over pigeons.

'It's so busy,' I say as I jump to dodge a determined group of French schoolchildren who seem intent on knocking me clean over. After being in sleepy Veganze for a couple of months I've forgotten what city life is like.

'This is nothing. Wait until you see the place in July,' comments Roberto. Suddenly, I feel ebullient with the thought of being in Italy in July; this is an enormous relief. Recently I've started to dread the thought of seeing through the month, let alone a lifetime, here. All at once, standing in the middle of this thriving hub, surrounded by noise, chaos and fun, holding the hand of my husband, I feel safe and secure. This is how I imagined our time in Italy would be. I've been so silly thinking about Chuck all the time. I've got that completely out of proportion. We're just going to be pals.

'Shall we take a look around the amphitheatre?' I suggest.

Roberto agrees, although he must have visited it on at least a dozen other occasions. He acts as guide, telling me that the amphitheatre was built in the first century AD and that in the thirteenth century an earthquake destroyed the majority of the exterior arcade but remarkably most of the interior is still intact. We climb up the steeply pitched tiers of pinkish marble seats to enjoy the dizzying views from the top. He holds my hand the entire way, even when it starts to get a bit damp with the effort of the climb.

'It's so wonderful here,' I gush as I flop down on to my bottom and take a moment to catch my breath.

'We should come here for the opera,' says Roberto. I nod enthusiastically, although I'd much prefer a pop concert or even a jazz festival. I don't want to admit as much in case I break the moment; he's trying to be thoughtful and attentive.

We pause for a few minutes. We're sitting facing in the direction the Romans would have faced when they were killing

Christians. The thought unnerves me and so I get up and wander to catch a view of the city. Roberto is right by my side.

'Verona it is the largest city in mainland Veneto. Most of the historic heart of Verona is enclosed in a loop of the river Adige,' he says, pointing out the loop in case I'm a total idiot and can't make it out for myself. I can see wonderful churches and other historical buildings scattered liberally throughout the higgledy-piggledy streets. I know we should go and visit one or two of those, Roberto would like it, but my eye is irresistibly drawn to the streets packed with pedestrians, which are bound to be the ones with the best shopping.

'Is that a market?' I try to keep my tone neutral but I do love a bargain. Roberto knows this. He grins and says, 'We can shop if you want to.'

I don't need to be invited twice. I scramble down the steps at quite some speed and in a matter of minutes I'm in the throng of the pedestrian-only street, which is flanked by tempting and elegant shops. Roberto buys a shirt and I buy a new bag. I don't need it and I already have one in the same colour but it's a different shape and the leather smells delicious. The bag is an indulgence, rather than a necessity, and all the more welcome for that.

We head north towards Piazza delle Erbe and we stumble into the market that I spotted from the amphitheatre. There are stalls selling fruit and veg, clothes, belts, shoes and a vast amount of tourist tat. It's the tourist tat that catches my eye because I'm entirely powerless in situations such as these. It's bizarre but true that whenever I'm on holiday I find snow globes and commemorative tea towels become my 'must have' items. I can't explain or excuse myself; under other circumstances I'm quite rational and stylish. I've learnt that as I can't control my foible, it's best to indulge it. I buy a handful of postcards and, as this is the city of love, I'm drawn to the stalls selling hundreds of red hearts. There are papier-mâché hearts, straw hearts, wooden ones and right at the centre of the stall, hanging far away from grasping hands, there are red glass hearts. They dangle on pretty red ribbons, swaying in the breeze, waiting to be selected like wallflower virgins at the school disco.

'Let's buy one. Or maybe two,' I suggest.

Fern has moved to LA with rock star Scott. That's a new begin-
ning which will guarantee the fairy-tale happy ending. Won't it?
Find out in **Love Lies.**

We visit Disneyland, we go and watch the whales swimming, we visit the zoo and we go to the predictable (unmissable), if not slightly crude and tasteless, Hollywood Boulevard. There's a shockingly bad waxwork museum there. The models are all slightly out of focus, off-scale versions of American actors. It's not a patch on Madame Tussaud's. I once had my photo taken with Scott's model in Madame Tussaud's in London but I don't confess to it. He knows I was a fan before I met him, not a crazy fan but enough of a fan. Yet confessing to the fact that I was sad enough to pose with a glorified candle would seem weird now. I'll have to find that photo and get rid of it. Knowing it exists sort of says I was half in love with Scott before I met him, which is bothersome.

We also visit the Guinness Book of Records Museum, where being a freak is celebrated; God Bless America. I insist that we go to Grauman's Chinese Theatre and take pictures. I'm desperate to put my hands and feet in the prints of Sophia Loren and Susan Sarandon. Scott is reluctant.

'I'm not mad about actors,' he says.

'Why's that then?'

'The people who make it their business to be vicious about me say that's because I've never been offered a role on the silver screen and I'm consumed with vulgar jealousy. It's nothing as crass. I just don't think they should be paid such obscene amounts for doing what the rest of us do all the time for free.'

He says this so casually that I almost miss the importance of what he's saying. Poor Scott, he certainly has come across more than his fair share of fakers and I suppose he does have to perform for strangers a lot of the time. 'Everyone isn't acting *all* the time,' I point out encouragingly. 'I'm not acting. You're not acting.'

Scott grins. 'OK, let's go to Grauman's then. You know I can't deny you anything.'

We spend a lot of time on Sunset Boulevard. The road is massive. In fact all roads are unfeasibly long in the US; when I was first given someone's business card I thought the house number was a telephone number. Other than length, it is a surprisingly mundane road to look at. Despite this, the illustrious and celebrated regularly come here, not just to score drugs; it has history. Scott tells me that a part of Sunset is known as 'Guitar Row', due to the large number of guitar stores and music-industry-related businesses dotted about. He points out the legendary recording studios – Sunset Sound and United Western Recorders – and he takes me to the Whiskey, a club renowned for launching the Doors and where Elton John made his US debut.

We visit Johnny Depp's old nightclub, the Viper Room, but we don't stay long; nightclubs and addicts are an explosive brew. We move on to the Standard to eat chips at the twenty-four-hour restaurant; Leonardo DiCaprio and Cameron Diaz reportedly have shares in that establishment. We sit in a cosy booth and chat over the sound of ice being crushed as pomegranate margaritas are being prepared for other people. When I'm in the mood for champagne we pop to Chateau Marmont, a plush, fantastical hideaway, or we float in the clouds at the Sky Bar. All these celebrated hotels, with legendary bars, boast famous patrons. We (and a lot of other recognisable people) do our shopping at Ralph's supermarket, also on Sunset. The bread's good but the thrill for me is that I stood behind Drew Barrymore in the checkout queue. I'm secretly keeping a list detailing the famous people I've met or spotted. Besides Drew, I spotted Jennifer Aniston while dining at the Mondrian and I stood in the loo queue with Emily Blunt at Mel's (it's a diner that's celebrated for its customers – strike that, I meant to say its waffles, strike that, I did mean the customers). I sat at a sushi bar next to Anne Marie Duff. It all leaves me gasping with excitement. Scott keeps the best until last.

Just when I start to insist that I simply can't be any more impressed with the razzmatazz, glitz and notoriety, he takes me to Rodeo Drive.

I stand, mouth wide open, gaping in absolute awe. Rodeo Drive is truly dazzling. Everything shines; the expansive windows displaying breathtaking clothes and jewels, the dark, sleek cars, the blonde glossy women and even the older plump men who accompany them, shine. These men wear a uniform of the confident wealthy: pale-blue shirts, red ties and navy blazers with buffed buttons and cufflinks and enormous watches that . . . yes, you've guessed it . . . shine. The street is clean enough to eat your dinner off and every street lamp is decorated with hanging baskets full of pretty bougainvillea that gently sway in the breeze. I turn around and around in circles.

'Where should we start?' I gasp, craning my neck to take in the enormous, shiny buildings.

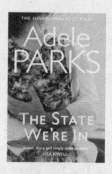

Take off with Jo, who is on a constant search to find the One, as she flies to Chicago in The State We're In.

I love airports. They combine – in abundance – three of my favourite things, *ever.* They're full of excitement (people are speeding off on wonderful holidays or to invigorating business meetings) and drama (people call out welcoming greetings or collapse into difficult goodbyes) and shops. Excitement, drama, shops, what's not to love? As I gaze around, I wonder how many momentous events are occurring in this very terminal, at this very second. How many declarations of love, how many hearts snapping?

I haven't taken a long-haul flight since before Martin and I split up. We used to travel together a lot; we visited New York, Thailand and Madrid. We planned to go on honeymoon to the Seychelles. I was so excited about that trip: tropical paradise islands, cobalt seas and endless white sand beaches; of course I was excited. I've often imagined since what that trip might have been like; it's impossible not to wonder. I bought three beautiful new bikinis, a floral beach bag and a huge straw sunhat especially. I spent weeks planning exactly what I'd look like lying under a parasol, the waves licking my toes, the gentle breeze brushing my limbs. After I called off the wedding, Martin came to some arrangement with the travel agent and exchanged our would-have-been-romantic honeymoon for a wild trip to Las Vegas with two of his mates. Word got back to me that for six days in a row he drank, gambled and passed out on dance floors.

I didn't indulge in anything similarly healing or commemorative. Swamped in the shame of knowing I'd hurt Martin severely and cost my parents a fortune, I didn't feel entitled to whiz away anywhere exotic, even though my friends and Lisa advised me that it would be a good idea. I've travelled since the split, but shorter distances. I've had three mini-breaks with three different boyfriends. Liam and I flew to Copenhagen; with Jamie I visited Rome; and it was Paris with Ben. I can't remember much about the airport from any of those trips, as on each occasion, I was consumed with giddy excitement. At least, I was on the outward journey; the returns were all considerably more downbeat. Truthfully, I probably do have a tendency to be a little bit too optimistic about the significance of a guy asking a woman to go on a mini-break; on each occasion I was devastated that a proposal wasn't forthcoming. I'm not saying that I'd have married any one of them, but I am saying I would have liked to be *asked* by one of them.

'Why do they even want to go abroad, if not to propose?' I asked Lisa forlornly after the third disappointment. I tend to think of Lisa – a married woman – as the font of all knowledge when it comes to stuff about men (but only if I like what she says). My sister just rolled her eyes and suggested, 'Great weather, food, architecture, or just to get drunk.'

'I know, I know there's all that stuff. I'd just enjoy it more if I thought it was to be shared on an ongoing basis,' I admitted forlornly. Then Lisa invited me along to a two-week all-inclusive family break in Spain.

'Won't I be in the way?' I asked.

'No, we see you as an on-tap babysitter,' Lisa replied; she wasn't entirely joking. That holiday was fun (noisy, chaotic and exhausting), and the huge beach bag finally came in useful for carrying spare nappies, blow-up beach balls and buckets and spades. But somehow it made me miss my honeymoon more not less.

OK, so. Onwards and upwards. Deep breath. It's essential that I approach this trip with some Zen-like thoughts. I have to put good karma out there, because obviously I am asking quite a lot of the universe in terms of return investment, I realise that. I have to be positive and calm. I need to be focused and determined. Truthfully I feel a dangerous mix between giddy with excitement and sick with nerves. I replay the conversation I had with Martin again and again in my head. If I think about my plan for any length of time I begin to feel a bit faint. The only possible answer is not to think about it for any length of time.

I thought she was my daughter.

I was wrong.

The
Stranger
in my
Home

The latest compelling novel from Adele Parks,
available now.

Read on for a preview. . .

Prologue

The doorbell rings.

I feel a flutter of excitement: is it what I've been waiting for? I rush to the door before the bell rings a second time and fling it open, but it's not what I'm expecting.

'Alison Mitchell?'

'Yes.'

It's something to do with the way he says my name, tentatively but somehow officially. 'Are you – look, I'm sorry. This is going to seem a bit peculiar.' He breaks off and looks to the ground, awkward. 'I just need to know, do you have a daughter who was born in St Mary's Hospital in Clapham between March 27th and 29th fifteen years ago?'

'Yes. Katherine; her birthday is the 27th.' I'm so used to being honest and straightforward that I splutter out this response before I consider whether this is the sort of info that should be routinely exchanged, on the doormat, with a total stranger. He swaps his expression of awkwardness for one of panic. 'Is Katherine in some sort of trouble?' I ask, fearful.

His mouth twists as though the words he has to spit out taste foul. 'Can I come in? This isn't something we can talk about on the doorstep.'

Fifteen Years Ago

*T*he smell of hospital disinfectant and her own blood lingered in the air, but she hardly noticed. They swaddled the mewling, delicate baby and placed her in Alison's outstretched arms. As she took hold and folded the small bundle into her, she knew that this is what her arms had ached for for so long.

People came and went: the nurses popped by to help her into a clean nightie, check she was comfortable; Jeff floated in and out of the ward, dashing off to make euphoric phone calls to family and friends, returning to relay their messages of joy and their congratulations. Alison and the baby were still, steady. They locked eyes – held each other's gaze and hearts – until the baby's lids grew heavy and sleep took hold. Even when the baby slept Alison couldn't tear her eyes away. She was so perfect. Alison gently moved aside the blanket so she could gaze at her child's legs, her arms, kiss the crook of her elbow and her butter-soft toes. She slept on and Alison continued to stare, mesmerised. It was love. Pure, unadulterated, unconditional, unending.

She had had an especially easy birth. In her birth plan she'd specified that she'd try any and all drugs to ease the pain and that she'd have a Caesarean if the experts thought that was the route to go; she trusted them to make the decision: they had the experience. As it happened, none of that was necessary; the baby took only four hours to arrive from

241

start to finish as though keen to make her way into the world. Jeff smuggled in a mini-bottle of Moët. They secretly drank it together from plastic cups pinched from the water fountain. Naturally, he had the lion's share; Alison managed just a couple of mouthfuls, as she fretted it would affect her milk. Under most circumstances, she'd have been discharged late that afternoon, but she was allowed to stay in hospital overnight. She'd been chatting to the nurses during labour – it really had been that comfortable – and told them she'd only just started her maternity leave the day before. She'd thought she might go back to work at some point and so she'd left it as late as possible before stopping, planning to maximise her time off with her baby, although from the moment she gave birth she guessed that had been unnecessary. She would never go back. Others might think that the mediocrity of her career and her paltry pay meant it wasn't worth her while. The truth was, it was the amount she worshipped Katherine that meant it couldn't be worth her while. She didn't want to miss a moment.

She'd had ambitious, unrealistic nesting plans. In the two weeks she'd allotted between stopping work and the due date, she'd planned to have new windows put in the house. The rattling ones were not good enough now they were to have an infant at home. She knew the timing of her plans was tight but she had thought she was in control. The baby showed her she wasn't by appearing eleven days early. The big relief was that their daughter was completely healthy, weighing in at an impressive seven pounds, two ounces; the nurses joked about how big she might have been if she'd gone full term! Still, Jeff had to rush home to chivvy along the window fitters and he returned crestfallen; the house was freezing, and the glaziers couldn't possibly complete the job in a day. They said, at the hospital, as they weren't busy, Alison could have the bed for the night; stay in for observation. They were doing her a favour. A kindness. The nurses insisted the baby went to the nursery because Alison almost fell to sleep holding her. They said she needed her rest.

'Do you know, killer-whale and bottlenose-dolphin calves don't sleep

for a whole month after they're born and, therefore, neither do their mothers?' Jeff informed the nurses.

'But the mother of your baby is not a killer whale,' they replied with mock-sternness. In fact, the midwife and the nurses were charmed by Jeff, by Alison, by the baby. An easy birth, a besotted mum, a supportive dad, a beautiful, healthy baby. So much bonhomie swilled around the ward you could smell it on the bouquets, hear it in the cries, the mewlings, the laughter, taste it in the cosy cups of tea.

They carried her away into the nursery, where there were a number of bassinets, a number of newborn babies.

Each one of these tiny, seemingly inconsequential acts sets destinies.

They brought the baby to her three times in the night. By the third time Alison barely opened her eyes; she was surprised at the depth of sluggishness her body had dived into, following the euphoria of the birth. She felt her daughter's head, then her cheek against her, then nuzzling, tugging. Hungry, animalistic rooting. She fastened so tightly to Alison's flesh and Alison wept with relief and delight. At last, at last.

Jeff returned to the hospital at eleven the next morning. He had the car seat and several sets of baby clothes because he wasn't sure which of the many squeezed into the little wardrobe Alison might prefer. She sensibly opted for a simple Babygro and a grey-and-white striped beanie hat; they could play with frills, bows and ribbons later.

'Darling, can you bear the idea of staying with my parents for a day or so? The house is so draughty, but the glaziers swear they'll be done by the end of the week.'

Alison nodded happily. She didn't care where she was, as long as she was with her baby. Her mother-in-law would be a help, she was sure of it. 'I feel sorry for you,' she said to Jeff as he kissed first the baby's head, then hers.

'Why's that?'

'Sleeping in that cold house, all alone last night, when we had each other to snuggle.' She brought the baby a fraction closer, kissed her cheek.

'I couldn't bear to miss a moment. She's changed already. Don't you think?' Jeff smiled and sort of shrugged. 'She seems a little longer, certainly smoother.'

He kissed Alison's head again. 'Maybe she's stretched out a bit. That's all the wonderful mothering you've been doing overnight. Now, are you going to feed her before we set off?'

'Yes, I think I'll try.' Again the baby latched on to Alison's breast with a natural ease which so many mothers would envy. She fed and fed until she wore a peculiar expression, a little like a satiated, happy drunk. She only, finally, let her mother go when her lids fluttered and closed and her small black hole of a mouth slipped to the side, when her cheeks were flushed and shiny with milk. Her dark eyelashes fanned out like a peacock's tail.

1

'**M**um? Mum, is that you?'

'Who else would it be? You should be asleep.' But as I say this I push my daughter's bedroom door and the hall light falls in a shaft across her room and lands on her bed. She's lying down but her eyes are bright and wide; she's beaming, holding an open book. This is how my fifteen year old rebels: she might occasionally read instead of turning the lights out. I know – I'm blessed.

'It's been a great day. Hasn't it?'

'It has,' I agree.

Lingering, for even a moment, is all the encouragement she needs; she scoots over to one side of the bed, allowing me room to sit down. I don't take much persuading, even though I know I ought to be insisting on lights out because there's school tomorrow and, because Jeff and I seem to have less and less time to ourselves as Katherine gets older, I ought to go downstairs and make time for him. However, mum–daughter pre-sleep chats have always been irresistible to me. It seems only five minutes since we'd lie on this bed, her infant body, warm and uninhibited, curled tightly into me, and I'd read *Each Peach Pear Plum* to her. Now I can't take such intimacy as an absolute given. Everything has to be continually renegotiated as she moves towards adulthood. I sit on the bed, then swing my legs up, lying flat and next to her now taut almost-woman body. I put my arm around her and she doesn't object; to my delight, she squirms closer. I've been gifted another day of her childhood. I live in fear of the moment when she shrugs me off and feel like punching the air every time I get away with the joy of dousing her in affection.

'What was your favourite bit of the match?' she asks.

'You winning,' I reply automatically. Her beam, which already stretched across her entire face, widens a fraction more. That was the right answer. It's always the right answer. Katherine, like all children, wants to know that her parents have noticed she's fabulous. That doesn't stop at five, fifteen or forty-five: it's eternal. She *is* fabulous, though, and I'm more than happy to chuck out endless compliments and affirmations. She scored two goals today; what a great start to the season. If she carries on like this then her team will certainly qualify for the finals of Rathbones National Schools Championship. I never played a team sport at school, let alone scored a winning goal. I live in awe of my talented daughter who, people say, might one day play lacrosse for GB.

Katherine starts to tell me what's going on in her book. It's set in a horrifying post-apocalyptic world, the sort that seems to fascinate so many teens. Some feisty heroine is plotting to murder a political tyrant in order to safeguard her family, who are all being exploited or tortured; it sounds pretty gory and a lot like the plot of the last book she read. I try to follow and show due interest but I can feel tiredness set into my limbs. It's not yet ten o'clock but I could fall to sleep here next to her.

Jeff puts his head around the door. 'I thought I'd find you in here.' I know he's mildly chastising me because he's itching to pour himself a gin and tonic and see what's new on Netflix. However, he's putty in Katherine's hands, too, and is also always up for a chat with her.

'We're just talking about the game.'

'You were extraordinary,' he says simply.

'Thanks, Dad.'

'You always are,' I add. Katherine grins and blushes with that complicated teen mix of pleasure and embarrassment, whilst she tries to turn the subject from her achievements.

'What's your book, Dad?' Jeff looks at the book in his hand. He appears to be somewhat surprised it's there, but we're not. He's a novelist and, when he's not sitting in front of his computer writing, then he is vociferously reading. He always has reading matter with him, it's as though it's surgically attached.

'It's about evolution.'

'Oh.' Katherine doesn't actually roll her eyes but I can tell she's not especially fascinated. Jeff apparently can't, or at least chooses not to, acknowledge her disinterest.

'You know what I've just read?' he says.

'What?' we chorus, humouring him. Since he reads so much, he has naturally become the self-appointed conveyer of interesting facts. His specialist subject is Mother Nature's mothers.

'Female octopuses lay between fifty thousand and two hundred thousand eggs at a time.'

'So many?' Katherine comments. As an only child, she's fascinated by how many siblings other people have, but even she must be overwhelmed by the thought of such a vast number.

'The mum ensures their survival by separating the eggs into groups based upon factors like size and shape. She then dedicates the next two months of her life to protecting them from predators and getting them enough oxygen by pushing water currents towards the eggs. Think of that – she actually tries to turn tides for her offspring.'

'Quite some dedication,' I remark.

'Amazing, isn't it? The thing is, she's so busy keeping them all alive, she doesn't have time to feed herself so she often ends up dying shortly after they hatch.'

'Er, thanks for that, Dad. I remember a time when all the stories you told me ended with "And they all lived happily ever after".' Katherine giggles and then rolls on to her side, effectively giving us leave to go downstairs.

As soon as we're on the landing, Jeff whispers, 'I've been to the garage, Alison, love, and bought Snickers.' When we are with Katherine we avoid eating the sort of snack that's laden with refined sugar; her diet is appropriate for an athlete, lots of protein and veg. 'G&Ts poured,' he adds; our diets are appropriate for a couple in their forties who have been together for ever and kindly refer to each other's excess pounds as 'love handles', 'something to grab on to' or 'more to love'; that's if we refer to them at all. We settle in front of our rather too-big flat-screen TV. Jeff says I can pick the film; I choose a political thriller I know he'll enjoy, because he did buy the king-size Snickers.

The thriller manages to hold about sixty per cent of my attention. A further thirty per cent of my mind is running through what I need to do tomorrow: what will I put in Katherine's packed lunch? Is her uniform clean and ironed? I must not forget to give her the cheque for the school trip to the theatre. The final ten per cent is wrapped up in acknowledging how damned lucky I am and offering up a silent prayer of thanks to whoever is listening, whoever I ought to be grateful to. People say that nothing is perfect and while, obviously, that's true – world peace continues to evade us, the queue you didn't choose will, inevitably, clear faster and even Kate Moss doesn't have a figure like Kate Moss any more – things are good for us. I never thought it could be like this. I'm thankful. Very, very thankful. I love Jeff. I love my daughter. I'm extremely lucky. I'm safe. That's what I tell everyone, over and over again, before they can jinx my excellent fortune with an envious glance or an irritated comment. *All right for some.* I'm lucky. *Safe.*

That's what I tell myself.

248

Have you read Adele's other enthralling novels?

Playing Away

Risking it all was exactly what she needed.
Connie has been happily married for a
year. But she's just met John Harding.
Imagine the sexiest man you can think
of. He's funny, disrespectful, fast, confident – and completely unscrupulous. He
is about to destroy Connie's peace of
mind and her grand plan for living
happily ever after with her loving
husband Luke. Written through the eyes
of the adulteress, *Playing Away* is the
closest thing you'll get to an affair
without actually having one.

Game Over

Would she ever meet a more worthy opponent?
Cas Perry doesn't want a relationship.
When her father walked out on her and
her mother she decided love and
marriage simply weren't worth the heart-
ache. Until she meets Darren. He
believes in love, marriage, fidelity and
constancy, so can he believe in Cas? Is
it possible the world is a better place
than she imagined? And if it is, after a
lifetime of playing games, is this
discovery too late?

LARGER THAN LIFE

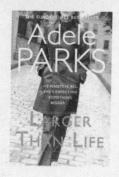

Georgina fell in love with Hugh the moment she first saw him. Unfortunately, he's someone else's husband and father. After years of waiting on the sidelines, Georgina finally gets him when his marriage breaks down. But her dream come true turns into a nightmare when she falls pregnant and Hugh makes it clear he doesn't want to do it all again. Georgina has to ask herself, is this baby bigger than the biggest love of her life?

THE OTHER WOMAN'S SHOES

Sexy and comfortable . . . Can you ever really have both?

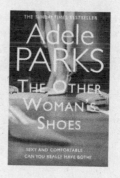

The Evergreen sisters have always been opposites with little in common. Until one day, Eliza walks out on her boyfriend the very same day Martha's husband leaves her. Now the Evergreen sisters are united by separation, suddenly free to pursue the lifestyles they think they always wanted. So, when both find exactly what they're looking for, everybody's happy . . . aren't they? Or does chasing love only get more complicated when you're wearing another woman's shoes?

Young Wives' Tales

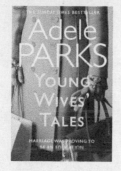

Marriage was proving to be an education.
Lucy stole her friend Rose's 'happily ever after' because she wanted Rose's husband – and Lucy always gets what she wants. Big mistake. Rose was the ideal wife and is the ideal mother; Lucy was the perfect mistress. Now neither can find domestic bliss playing each other's roles. They need more than blind belief to negotiate their way through modern life. And there are more twists in the tale to come. . .

Men I've Loved Before

She thought he was definitely the one. But what about the one before?
Nat doesn't want babies; she accepts this is unusual but not unnatural. She has her reasons; deeply private and personal which she doesn't feel able to share. Luckily her husband Neil has always been in complete agreement, but when he begins to show signs of changing his mind, Nat is faced with a terrible dilemma. Is the man she has married really the man she's meant to be with?

ABOUT LAST NIGHT

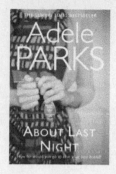

How far would you go to save your best friend?
There is nothing best friends Steph and Pip wouldn't do for one another. That is, until Steph begs Pip to lie to the police as she's desperately trying to conceal not one but two scandalous secrets to protect her family. Her perfect life will be torn apart unless Pip agrees to this lie. But lying will jeopardise everything Pip's recently achieved after years of struggle. It's a big ask. So what would you do?

WHATEVER IT TAKES

What if love's not enough?
How far would you go for the people you love? For Londoner Eloise Hamilton, there can be no greater sacrifice than uprooting to Dartmouth, leaving her perfect world so that her husband Mark can live his. But when a life-changing family secret emerges, Eloise suddenly finds herself struggling to hold everything together for the people she loves. Someone is bound to be overlooked, and the damage might be irreparable. . .

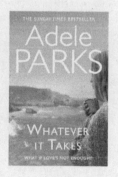

Spare Brides

No more waiting. It's time to live again. The 1920s: a time of hope, promise – and parties. But not all the men came home after The War. Meet the spare brides. Young, gorgeous – and unexpectedly alone. Into their circle comes angry, damaged, and dangerously attractive, Edgar Trent. He is an irresistible temptation. And the old rules no longer apply . . .

If You Go Away

Can he love her more than he hates war?
A moment's indiscretion causes debutante Vivian Foster's world to crumble just as the country around her erupts into a devastating war. Everything seems bleak. Until she meets celebrated playwright Howard Henderson. He wants no part killing a faceless enemy, but refusing to fight will lead to imprisonment, even death. Now they've found each other and something worth fighting for. But will the war demand that sacrificing their future together is the only way to honour their love?

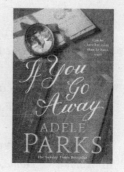

© Conrad Parks

Adele Parks worked in advertising until she published the first of her fifteen novels in 2000. Since then, her *Sunday Times* bestsellers have been translated into twenty-six different languages. Adele spent her adult life in Italy, Botswana and London until 2005 when she moved to Guildford, where she now lives with her husband and son. Adele believes reading is a basic human right, so she works closely with The Reading Agency as an Ambassador for Reading Ahead, a programme designed to encourage adult literacy.

Meet Adele! Visit her website for the latest
news on her upcoming events
www.adeleparks.com

Head to Facebook
for exclusive extras
**facebook.com/
OfficialAdeleParks**

Chat with Adele
on Twitter
@adeleparks